***This was no dream; this was real.
She was lying in bed cuddled up
to a preacher.***

"Good morning," she said, and then they stared
at each other until both their faces flushed with the
knowledge of where they were and how close they
were.

"I'm afraid I don't remember much about last
night," he said. "How did I get here?"

"You said you didn't want to go home, so I rescued
you."

He chuckled. "You rescued me?"

"Well, don't tell anybody. I don't want to ruin my
reputation."

"Your secret is safe with me."

She gave him a wicked smile. "And yours is safe
with me."

"Did anything happen here last night?"

"Believe me, Daniel, if anything had happened in
this bed last night, you'd remember."

Dear Reader,

Do I have a sweet lineup for you—just in time for Valentine's Day! What's more enticing than a box of chocolates? The answer lies in the next story, *Cordina's Crown Jewel*, from *New York Times* bestselling author Nora Roberts's CORDINA'S ROYAL FAMILY series. This gem features a princess who runs away from royal responsibility and straight into the arms of the most unlikely man of her dreams!

Another Valentine treat is Jackie Merritt's *Marked for Marriage*, which is part of the popular MONTANA MAVERICKS series. Here, a feisty bronco-busting beauty must sit still so that a handsome doctor can give her a healthy dose of love. And if it's heart-thumping emotion you want, Peggy Webb continues THE WESTMORELAND DIARIES series with *Bittersweet Passion*, a heavenly opposites-attract romance between a singing sensation and a very handsome minister hero.

In *With Family in Mind*, Sharon De Vita launches her gripping SADDLE FALLS miniseries. One Valentine's Day, this newlywed author admits, she wrote a heartwarming love poem to her husband about their first year together! Our next family tale is *Sun-Kissed Baby*, by Patricia Hagan—a darling tale of a new single mom who falls for the man she thinks is her little boy's father. This talented author shares her Valentine's Day dinner tradition with us—making "a heart-shaped meatloaf" and at the end of the pink meal, "a heart-shaped ice cream cake, frosted with strawberry whipped cream." The icing on the cake this month is Leigh Greenwood's *Undercover Honeymoon*, a passionate tale of two reunited lovers who join forces to stay ahead of a deadly enemy and care for an orphaned little girl.

Make sure that you sample every Special Edition delight this month has to offer. I wish you and your loved ones a warm and rose-filled Valentine's Day (and that box of chocolates, too)!

Best,

Karen Taylor Richman
Senior Editor

Please address questions and book requests to:
Silhouette Reader Service
U.S.: 3010 Walden Ave., P.O. Box 1325, Buffalo, NY 14269
Canadian: P.O. Box 609, Fort Erie, Ont. L2A 5X3

Bittersweet Passion

PEGGY WEBB

Silhouette®

SPECIAL EDITION™

Published by Silhouette Books

America's Publisher of Contemporary Romance

For Michael…
"Wonderful Tonight" and always…

 SILHOUETTE BOOKS

ISBN 0-373-24449-5

BITTERSWEET PASSION

Copyright © 2002 by Peggy Webb

This edition published by arrangement with Harlequin Books S.A.

® and TM are trademarks of Harlequin Books S.A., used under license.
Trademarks indicated with ® are registered in the United States Patent
and Trademark Office, the Canadian Trade Marks Office and in other
countries.

Visit Silhouette at www.eHarlequin.com

Printed in U.S.A.

PEGGY WEBB

and her two chocolate Labs live in a hundred-year-old house not far from the farm where she grew up. "A farm is a wonderful place for dreaming," she says. "I used to sit in the hayloft and dream of being a writer." Now, with two grown children and more than forty-five romance novels to her credit, the former English teacher confesses she's still a hopeless romantic and loves to create the happy endings her readers love so well.

When she isn't writing, she can be found at her piano playing blues and jazz or in one of her gardens planting flowers. A believer in the idea that a person should never stand still, Peggy recently taught herself carpentry.

Dear Daniel,

If your father were not in a coma, I know that he would be the first person you would turn to when it comes to matters of the heart. However, I am your mother and my sorrows will never take precedence over my children. I am here for you.

It is clear that you are deeply in love with Skylar. And rightly so—she is a very beautiful woman. So beautiful that it might be hard for you to see the pain in her eyes. Her father, a minister, just as you are, hurt her and died before they could make peace. Regardless of the love she feels for you, you are still a small reminder of the pain. So use your gift of love and forgiveness. And remember that she can run away, but she can never hide from love. True love has wings and will find her wherever she goes.

With all my love and understanding,

Mom

Prologue

From the diary of Anne Beaufort Westmoreland:

September 18, 2001

The doctor just came in and said, "Anne, I know this is going to be hard for you, but I'm afraid there's nothing else we can do here for Michael."

I was too stunned to ask questions. I was too scared to say, "You can't just give up hope." Too mad to scream, "What do you mean, nothing else you can do? You're a doctor. *Do something.*"

He patted my hand and left, saying he'd send somebody named Ethelene to talk to me about moving Michael to a nursing home.

What kind of person calls herself that? It makes me think of something that would burn up if you lit a match to it.

I can't believe this is happening to me.

Well, there I go again being selfish. Thinking only of myself when it's my husband I should be worried about. And oh, I am, I am. It's just that Michael's lying in his coma looking peaceful and relaxed while I'm left in the real world all by myself. Trying to cope.

Of course, I'm not by myself. I have my three children, and every single one of them would come if I called. I'm not going to, though. They have their lives. Emily is planning her wedding to Jake, Hannah's still chasing a story out in Yellowstone and Daniel has a big church in Atlanta looking to him for leadership.

No, I'll do this all by myself.

The first thing I'm going to do is tell Michael, "It's time to get up now, darling. Hurry before they kick us out of here."

I'll try to keep it light because I don't want to alarm him.

Or maybe I do. Maybe I'll scream at him, "Michael Westmoreland, if you don't get out of that bed this instant they're going to haul your butt out of here like a load of lumber and stick you in some godawful place where nobody expects you to leave. Ever."

Oh, I can't bear to think of it. I can't bear to think about a future without Michael. My heart, my soul, my life.

There has to be hope. I won't give up. I *won't*. And I won't let Michael give up either. Even if we do have to move into a nursing home.

I lean toward the bed, touch his hand and whisper, "Michael, wake up, darling."

But he doesn't move. Doesn't blink. Doesn't respond in any way.

After he first got hit by that avalanche in the Himalayas I was able to feel his thoughts. I knew that Michael was somewhere listening to me, feeling me, knowing me.

I'm not sure anymore. Though, God forbid I should tell any of the children that. Emily is convinced her father will wake up in time to walk down the aisle and give her away. And Daniel's faith never wavers.

"We just have to keep praying, Mom," he tells me, and oh, I know it's true. But sometimes I wonder if God's really listening. Maybe there's too much static. Just think...millions of people sending up petitions, all of them desperate.

Like me.

Well, there now. I've said it. I'm feeling desperate. And alone. I need to cry. I need to scream. I need help.

God, help me...

A loud ringing. I jump as if I'm shot. It's the phone. Is it more bad news? Maybe I won't even answer it.

Chapter One

"Hello, Mom."

The minute Daniel spoke, his mother started to cry, and the sense of foreboding he'd had all morning grew. That was why he'd picked up the phone in the first place. He usually waited until after he'd checked his messages with the church's secretary before calling the hospital in Vicksburg to find out if there was news from home. But something had kept prodding him, something dark and urgent.

"Mom? What's wrong? Is it Dad?"

"Yes...no, not what you're thinking. Oh, Daniel, the doctors are sending him to a nursing home."

"When?"

"Soon. As soon as arrangements are made for the transfer. Probably first thing next week."

"I'll be there."

"No...no, I can handle this. Really, I can."

"You don't have to go through this alone. I'll *be* there, Mom."

"Oh, Daniel...they say there's nothing else they can do." Her voice gave a little hitch, then she sniffed two or three times before coming back on the phone. "I'm sorry. I'm such a mess."

"You're tired. Anyone would be after four months of caretaking. There's nothing to apologize for. You're entitled to express your feelings. It's not only human, it's healthy."

"No wonder all your parishioners love you so much. You're a marvelous minister, Daniel. I'm so proud of you. And Michael was...*is,* too. I want you to know that."

"Not everybody in my flock finds me as appealing as a mother does, but thanks for your vote of confidence.... I'll drive over after Sunday morning services, Mom...to help you take care of things."

"What about Sunday evening services?"

"Quentin can take care of that."

"You're sure?"

"That's what assistant pastors are for."

After Daniel had hung up he tried not to think about why he would be going back to Mississippi. Instead he made arrangements with Quentin, then called his secretary Evelyn in to reschedule his Monday and Tuesday appointments.

His plan was to be back in Atlanta in time for Wednesday-night meditations.

The day they moved Michael into the nursing home, it was pouring rain, a gray cheerless day perfectly suited for their somber task. Daniel kept his dark thoughts to himself. As a matter of fact, he tried hard to erase them completely.

He tried hard to pretend an optimism he was far from feeling. For his sake as well as his mother's.

Lately he'd felt a slipping away inside himself, a loosening of truths long held to be inviolable. He'd tried to pass his feelings off as fatigue due to overwork and stress, but they were manifesting themselves with increasing regularity. This scared him more than he cared to admit.

He was a minister. A man whose faith was supposed to be unassailable. In addition, he was now the head of the Westmoreland family with a mother and two sisters looking to him for leadership.

Michael had been the cornerstone on which their family was built, the rock they'd all stood on, the bulwark they'd all been sheltered by. And now it was Daniel's turn.

Heavenly Father, make me adequate to the task, he silently prayed, but his words seemed hollow even to himself.

Anne was at Michael's bed adjusting the pillow, smoothing the covers, touching his face, her gestures jerky, her chatter nervous.

"Everything's going to be all right, Michael," she said. "You'll see. We're going to like this place. See, they have a big window with a view of the front lawn. There's a magnolia tree out there, and a bird feeder. Even a little pond. Much better than looking out at the hospital parking lot...don't you think so, Daniel?"

She turned to him in something as close to desperation as he'd ever seen in his mother. He put his arm around her and drew her to a chair.

"I do. The view is great, and when the sun shines we'll open the window so Dad can smell the grass and listen to the birds."

"I hadn't thought of that. He's missing the outdoors. I *know* he is."

"Maybe that's exactly what he needs to trigger an awakening."

"Yes, yes. And the staff here is very nice. Don't you think so?"

So far they'd only met three people, the director Winslow Raines, the daytime head nurse Sally Schuster, and the physical therapist Gloria Marshall. Raines was a jovial Santa look-alike, Schuster a dour spinster who looked as if she'd take scalps if you crossed her and Marshall a freckled sprite who looked twelve instead of three times that.

"I do. I think we're going to like it here."

His mother held on to Daniel's hand, and they lapsed into a silence as they both watched the bed where Michael lay, watched and waited. Hoping for a miracle.

Daniel had been praying for one since June, battering Heaven's gate with his fervent petitions, imploring his Father to bend a compassionate ear his way, to turn a tender heart toward Vicksburg and restore a beloved husband and father to his family.

So far he'd received no answers. Or had he? What if the answer was *no?*

Unconsciously he balled his hands into fists. He couldn't accept that. Not yet. His mother was counting on him.

"I need to go home for a little while, wash up, eat a bite, get some things for tonight," she said. "Will you stay here until I get back?"

"Of course. Why don't you let me stay tonight, too? You need some rest."

"Michael's counting on me. I can't let him spend his first night in a new place without me."

Daniel knew it was no use to argue. Instead he kissed his mother's forehead, then escorted her to the door. She cupped his cheek briefly, then was gone. Before he was even settled into the chair, she was back standing at the bed bending over Michael.

"I'll be back soon, darling." She kissed him softly on the lips, then wagged two fingers at Daniel as she left.

Daniel went to the window and watched until she drove out of the parking lot, then he stood at the bed looking down at his father. Michael had lost weight. His pajamas hung on him and his swarthy sun-and-snow-burned skin had lightened to a pale gold that looked yellow in the waning light of day.

This was Daniel's favorite time of day. He flicked off the lights then stood in the deepening shadows and listened in the stillness.

Sounds during this time of day became sharper, clearer—the distant squeaking of rubber wheels against polished tiles, the faint clinking of silver as dinner trays were dispersed to the rooms, the ping of rain against the windowpanes.

Daniel closed his eyes and fell into evening, absorbing the place, centering himself. And then suddenly, there was music. The voice of an angel. Sweet and clear. A glorious golden contralto lifted in song.

Spellbound, Daniel listened. He couldn't make out the words. But, ah…the melody. It rang through him as if the angels themselves were pulling at his heartstrings.

He was so enthralled he didn't even hear the door open. He didn't know anyone was in the room until the woman spoke.

"Reverend Westmoreland? May I turn the light on?"

"Of course. I'm sorry."

He snapped the light on and there stood a large beaming woman, her face as shiny as patent leather shoes.

"I've brought you some dinner, Reverend," she said, and when she smiled she showed two gold teeth.

"Thank you..." He looked at the name tag. "Mrs. Strong. But you didn't have to do that."

The angel's voice lifted pure and rich down the hall, and Daniel realized he was hungry.

"It's no problem, Reverend. I take good care of my patients and their families. I want you to know that."

"We appreciate that. And please...call me Daniel."

She smiled again, that warm gold-toothed smile that brightened the room. "If you call me Vicky we'll be all set here."

Beyond his room the voice sailed upward on a clear sustained note, then abruptly dropped back an octave to a deep intimate tone that made the hair rise on the back of Daniel's neck.

"It's a deal," he said.

"All right then, I'll leave you to your supper. It's ham and greens. Good country cooking. We've got a good cook here."

The beautiful voice dropped even lower in a dark bluesy riff that had Daniel wondering why his collar was too tight and the room too hot.

"Wait," he said as Vicky headed toward the door. "Who is that singing?"

"Oh, that. That's Skylar, Skylar Tate. I'll go tell her to stop if it's bothering you."

"No, no, please. It's..." *Riveting. Mind-boggling. Miraculous.* "...very nice." He had to know more. "Is she a patient here?"

Vicky laughed. "Lord, no. That girl's got more energy than any three of us put together. Healthy as a horse. She just comes here when she's in town to entertain our patients. They all seem to like it."

"No doubt."

"But now if she ever gets too loud for you, you just let

me know. I'll tell her to pipe down. I don't know if she'll do it, though.'' Vicky laughed. ''The last time I did that, way back last Easter I think, when that mean old Mr. Gumpus was still here, Skylar just laughed and said, 'Vicky, you tell that old fuddy-duddy to go straight to hell'... Oh, excuse me, Reverend...I didn't mean to offend you.''

Daniel laughed. ''The only thing that offends me is when people start treating me as if I'm not human like everyone else.''

''Well, now, that's a relief. No, more than that. It's a pure-dee jubilee.''

''What's a jubilee, Vicky?''

''It's joy that just pops up out of nowhere, usually in the least likely of places.''

''Sounds great. I'll have to look for some.''

''Oh, it won't come if you go looking. You have to wait and let it come to you...'night, Daniel.''

''Goodnight.'' She left, pulling the door closed behind her. ''Oh, Vicky...would you mind leaving the door open?''

She gave him a knowing grin. ''Sure thing, Rev.''

His dinner tray forgotten, Daniel gave himself over to the heavenly music. With the cessation of conversation and the door wide open he began to make out snatches of lyrics. A smile spread across his face that got bigger and bigger.

Skylar Tate was singing about honky-tonks, wild wicked women and blues-struck men with empty whiskey glasses and empty beds.

Drifting toward the door like a moth to a flame, Daniel revised his opinion about the singer. He pictured a fallen angel. With a crooked halo...and spike-heeled shoes.

The door down the hall had opened and there she was. In stiletto heels. Red. A skirt so short it barely covered the subject. Black. A little scarlet sweater that left not much to the imagination and lush lips the color of ripe plums.

He guessed he was staring. Skylar Tate stared right back, hip slung, one eyebrow arched. Long, long legs. The blackest hair he'd ever seen. Lots of it. Hair that inspired fantasies. Not the tame kind where he was running his hands through it, but the bawdy kind where he was watching her bent over him with her raven's hair spreading across his thighs.

A lazy satisfied cat's smile spread across Skylar Tate's face. As if she knew. As if she could read his mind.

And why not? A woman such as that was bound to know the effect she had on men.

And Daniel was all man. In spite of what some of his parishioners thought.

Lord, if they knew what he was thinking right now the ladies of the altar guild would hold a prayer meeting for him. The organist would have a heart attack. The pastor/parish relations committee would run him out of Atlanta on a rail.

The gorgeous fallen angel was still smiling at him with wicked glee. What was he supposed to say? To do?

Lord, he'd been so wrapped up in his profession, so caught up in his father's coma that he didn't even remember what it was like to strike up a conversation with a pretty woman, let alone approach one.

What would he say? "Hi, I'm the Reverend Westmoreland, and you inspire me to sin?"

Suddenly Skylar Tate began to move. She was coming straight toward him. Her hips...Lord, have mercy. He'd never seen anything like it. The way she moved would make saints turn in their halos.

She was closer now, so close he could see that her eyes

were so blue they were almost purple. Would she stop when she got to his father's room? Would she speak to him?

His mouth got dry and his tongue felt glued to his throat. He was so hot he could feel his shirt sticking to him in damp patches.

Now he could see the heart-shape of her lips. A tiny black mole just above the right side where they still curved upward. And suddenly he knew why they called it a beauty mark. Was it real?

It had to be. Everything about her looked real. She wasn't the kind of woman given to posturing. He could tell.

He cleared his throat, mentally rehearsing what he was going to say when Skylar Tate drew even with the door, practicing the way he did with his Sunday sermons. Except this was no sermon he planned to deliver. Not by a long shot.

He was thinking of something along the lines of, "Good evening." Or perhaps, "Hello. How are you?" Brilliant repartee. Sure to bowl her over.

She was almost here. He could smell her fragrance. Something warm and sweet and dark. Gardenias growing in a deep jungle.

The sweat was now soaking his collar.

Then all of a sudden she was standing right in front of him.

"Hi, there." Her voice was rich and throaty. Mesmerizing. Sexy. "You don't look like a preacher."

How did she know that? Did it show? Did preachers wear some kind of label that was invisible to themselves but glowed like neon to beautiful women? Did fallen angels have special radar that detected men of the cloth the same way trained dogs sniffed out bombs?

His tongue clove to the roof his mouth, and he was still

trying to pry it off when Skylar Tate gave him one more wicked smile, then walked on down the hall.

Still, Daniel hadn't said a word. Not one.

As embarrassed as if he were thirteen and had just been awakened by his first wet dream, he slid back into the shadows of his father's room.

And all he could think of was that the back of Skylar Tate looked just as good as the front of her.

Chapter Two

Skylar had rung like bells when she stopped in front of Daniel Westmoreland, and she was still tingling when she got to the parking lot. Her condition made her so mad she kicked her back tire, then she kicked it again, just for good measure.

"Damn, damn, damn," she said, then she added "Hellfire," on general principles.

She wouldn't touch a preacher with a ten-foot pole. Nosiree, bob. She wouldn't touch one with a twenty-nine-and-a-half-foot pole. That's what she'd always told herself. She'd grown up in that particular fishbowl, a preacher's kid, wild, willful and rebellious, the talk of the town, the most spectacular failure of her father's long and illustrious career.

On her twenty-first birthday he'd called her up. She'd been out in Las Vegas at the time, bumming around, taking singing gigs wherever she could find them.

"I'm in the business of saving souls, Skylar, and it pains me to know that I haven't been able to save yours."

That's what he'd said. Without preamble. Without even wishing her a happy birthday.

"Do you know what day this is?" she'd asked, and he'd said, "Of course. You're an adult now. That's why I'm so worried about you."

"Well, the next time just send a card, Daddy."

The year after that she'd been in Alaska backpacking with Rick Savory on her birthday, and the next year in Europe singing with the newly formed band, New Blues. The band had returned to America to a modest amount of acclaim and a new record contract that had booted them up the ladder a bit. And if they weren't on the rungs of roaring success, at least they were close enough.

One of Skylar's biggest regrets was that her daddy hadn't lived to see her perform. He'd have been mortified.

Her parents had been killed in a car accident while she was in Europe, and nobody had told her until after the funeral. Maybe it was because they didn't know where to find her, Reverend Wayne Tate's black-sheep daughter. Or perhaps they hadn't even tried. Perhaps they'd thought she'd be an embarrassment to the good Reverend Tate as he strolled through the Pearly Gates and looked back at his send-off.

Skylar climbed into her ancient Thunderbird convertible and roared home with the top down, breaking the speed limits. She was still fuming when she turned into her parents' driveway.

Funny, that's how she still thought of the little cottage she'd inherited, even after five years. Her parents' house. And in a way she guessed it still was. She hadn't changed anything, not even the faded drapes.

Why bother? She was on the road most of the time anyhow. It was only a place to hang her hat between tours.

Pussy Willow came to greet her, the cat she'd rescued from a back alley in Toronto four years earlier. She curled herself around Skylar's ankles purring, but even that didn't lift her from her blue funk.

It was all Daniel Westmoreland's fault. Why did he have to be a preacher?

She picked her cat up and carried her to the sofa where she plopped down and kicked off her shoes.

"I made a fool of myself today, Miss Pussy W.," she said, and the cat batted at her hair. "You want to know? I thought so. Well, when I got to the nursing home today I saw this *gorgeous* man get out of his car…Georgia license plates, mind you, and I thought, hmmm, somebody new and interesting has come to town, somebody I can have fun with.

"Well, I inquired of old battle-ax, you know that horsefaced nurse Schuster, and she told me who he was, told me all about him, in fact."

Pussy Willow sat up and waited with her tail switching.

"Waiting for the punch line, are you? Well, I'm not going to keep you in suspense. He's a preacher."

The cat sniffed her disdain, then leapt off Skylar's lap.

Skylar got up and padded barefoot to the stereo, put on a great Eric Clapton CD and began to dance. Transported by the music she unbuttoned her sweater and tossed it onto a high-backed chair. Next came her skirt. Then her black lace thong.

It was only when Pussy Willow jumped onto the back of the sofa to watch a bird out the window that Skylar remembered to pull down the shades.

"What the heck," she told her cat, laughing. "Might as

well give the neighbors a thrill. Some of them could use loosening up.''

Daniel was lifting the cover off his dinner when he heard a familiar voice.

''Yahoo, is anyone home?'' His mother's friend Clarice stuck her head around the door frame, and seeing him, grinned. ''Daniel! Come here you old sweetpea.''

She hugged him, then plopped an oversize purse on the floor and marched toward the bed like a brass band, bangle bracelets clanking, high-heeled boots clicking, the beads around her neck bouncing.

''Hello, Michael, I'm here to bring a little fun into your life. The three of us are having a spend-the-night party tonight, just you and me and Anne. If I were you I'd get out of that bed so I could defend myself.''

Daniel was delighted to learn she'd be spending the night, though he was not surprised. His mother's friends were not merely cheerleaders when things were good but soldiers when things went bad.

''I'm glad you're staying tonight, Clarice. That's very generous-hearted of you.''

She settled into a chair, her full skirt billowing about her, a tiny, trim woman who was still gorgeous at fifty-six, which could account for her five husbands. That, plus her personality. She made you feel good just being around her.

''Ha! I have ulterior motives. Have you seen the director here? Sexy as all get-out, even if he is slightly roly-poly...and speaking of sexy, have you met Skylar Tate yet?''

Clarice knew practically everybody, and loved to tell what she knew. And Daniel was more than curious about Skylar Tate.

''I saw her. Do you know her?''

"She's from Huntsville, a good old Alabama girl, grew up practically at my back door. She was always a wild little thing, climbing trees, skinning her knees, running off so she could hang around the honky-tonks listening to the music."

"She sounds full of spirit."

"Oh, she was, still is, though how that happened is a mystery to me. She was saddled with the worst set of god-awful parents who ever drew a breath."

"Abusive?"

If Clarice had said yes, Daniel was going to drive over to Huntsville and personally beat the hell out of them, he who had never wanted to lay a hand on anybody in his life.

"No, just narrow-minded, anal-retentive bigots who never met a human being they thought worthy of love, even their own daughter. No wonder she ran away."

"How old was she?"

"Sixteen the first time. They brought her back, but the second time she left—she was eighteen—they didn't even try to bring her home. Then the Reverend Tate got transferred here, and I lost touch for a few years till I married Sam and moved here myself. You remember him? My fourth husband."

"Yes, I do. I always liked Sam."

What he really wanted to talk about was Skylar's father, the minister. But Clarice was already reminiscing about Sam.

"So did I. He had a wonderful smile, and one of the biggest...oh well, you don't want to hear that. What you're wanting to hear about is Skylar Tate."

"It shows, huh?"

"Honey, any man who has ever met her wants to know more about her. She's living right here in Vicksburg, at least when she's not on the road."

"On the road?"

"Performing. She's the lead singer for the New Blues."

"That explains the voice. Unforgettable."

Anne walked in and conversation shifted away from Skylar, but Daniel couldn't forget her. On the drive back to Belle Rose he decided to take a detour by the mall. He needed to pick up some shaving cream...and a book wouldn't hurt, something to read during all those lonely hours sitting at the nursing home.

But you're going back to Atlanta tomorrow, aren't you?

That had been his plan, of course, but he hated to leave his mother the day after they put Michael into the nursing home. He'd call Quentin and ask him to cover one more day.

Daniel was whistling when he walked into the mall, and the first thing he spotted was a music store. Why not? He walked the aisles, browsing through CDs with names that sounded like something you'd want to stamp out from the pulpit if you were that kind of minister. Thank God, he wasn't.

Finally he approached the pimply-faced young man at the front and asked, "Do you have anything by Skylar Tate?"

"Oh, yeah. Man, she's some hot chick. Have you seen her video?"

"Video?"

"Music video. *Too Hot to Handle.*"

That's how Daniel ended up back at Belle Rose with no shaving cream and no book, but six CDs and a music video of Skylar Tate.

He slid the music video into the machine then leaned back against his headboard to watch. A single spotlight shone on a dark stage, then as a moaning blues riff filled the air, the spotlight brightened and there was Skylar Tate, head down, long black hair covering her face and her torso, nothing showing but a pair of tight tiny black shorts and long, long legs.

She started to sing, then flipped her head back, and Daniel came up off the bed. At first he thought she was wearing nothing at all except shorts, and then he saw the glitter of sequins, a random string or two. It could hardly be called a top. Not even a bra. More like a set of pasties on strings.

Riveted, he stood in front of the TV. And when it was over, he rewound the tape and watched the whole thing again.

By the time it was finished he had to stand a while and compose himself before he could walk. Finally he went to the bathroom and splashed cold water over his face and neck. When that wasn't enough, he jerked off his clothes and climbed into the shower. The water was so cold it stung.

Daniel stayed until he could feel goose bumps all over himself, then he climbed into bed, turned off the light and lay there with his eyes wide open.

The next morning Daniel woke up with the vague feeling of something amiss. He lay still listening to the birdsong outside his window, the familiar ticktock of the grandfather clock in the hallway and the comforting whirring of the ceiling fan above his bed.

"All's well," he said, then climbed out of bed to shave. Using a bar of soap. He nicked himself on the chin and had to staunch the flow of blood with a piece of toilet paper.

With the paper still sticking to his chin he walked out onto the balcony, gazed out over the garden and listened. Merely listened. A brisk breeze stirred the trees, and a squirrel making his way to the bird feeder hung on while the branch danced underneath him. Nearby two mocking-birds dive-bombed his head, scolding and flapping their wings.

And above it all, the sun. Painting the morning skies.

Daniel wasn't on his knees, but he was praying. For the first time in weeks.

He stayed on the balcony a while longer, and when he went inside he knew what he had to do. Picking up the phone he called Atlanta.

Skylar didn't usually go to the nursing home two days in a row. She also didn't go early. Mornings she reserved for herself, for leisurely baths with lots of candles burning and scented oil poured into the water, for lazy breakfasts in the garden with her face turned up to the sun, the only music the sound of birds, for long walks in the little park down the street, for sitting on the porch swing reading a good book.

Then why was she standing barefoot at her closet trying to decide what to wear to Tranquility Manor?

Don't think about it, she told herself. In fact, that summed up her whole life. *Move. Do something. Run. But don't think. Never think.*

She put on tight black capris, a little yellow sweater and drop-dead shoes with four-inch heels and rhinestone straps across her toes.

The first thing she noticed when she got to the nursing home was the car with the Georgia license plates. That brought a big smile to her face.

She was still smiling when she went through the front door where Bob Clements, the janitor, was mopping the tiles.

"Good morning, Bob."

"'Morning, Miss Skylar. Better watch your step, floor's slick."

"How's Harriet today?" Harriet was Bob's wife and a resident in the nursing home. Almost blind from diabetes, and with one leg amputated.

"Better, thank you. She sure does look forward to your visits. They cheer her up considerably."

"I'm glad."

"You stayin' in town long this time, Miss Skylar?"

"That all depends, Bob."

On what, she didn't exactly know. The band wouldn't go on tour again until spring. They had a big Christmas concert in Huntsville, but, other than that, Skylar was free.

A little voice inside her scoffed, *Free?*

She lengthened her stride, trying to outrun the voice…and ran smack into the Reverend Daniel West-moreland. She probably would have toppled off her shoes if he hadn't caught her.

And held on.

And it felt good. Too good.

"Whoa, there." He smiled down at her, and she melted all the way down to her rhinestones. He had the kind of smile that would call angels from the heavens…if you believed in such things. Which she definitely did not, in spite of all her father's efforts.

"It's a good thing I was here to catch you," he said.

"Hmmm, it's a very good thing."

Daniel's hands were still on her shoulders, and his body was too close for comfort.

Or maybe not close enough. Skylar shifted closer, so close her hips brushed against him.

Sooo, the reverend is all man, is he?

She gave him a wicked knowing smile, then instantly wished she hadn't. He stepped back quickly, his smile fading, and in its place was a look of genuine confusion.

Dammitdammitdammit.

"I'm sorry," he said. "I didn't mean to overstep my bounds."

Now she was getting mad. Whether at him or herself, she didn't know. All she knew was that she wanted to lash out.

She knew better than to get involved with a preacher. Even for a two-minute chat in the hallway in front of Bob and Nurse Hatchet-face and anybody else who happened to be passing by.

It just simply wasn't safe. Especially when the preacher looked as good as Daniel Westmoreland.

And so she was fixing to say something that would make him run as far and as fast as possible. Something that would disgust and shock him so much she'd be rid of him forever. No more temptation in her path. No more lying awake at night wondering about possibilities.

"Why, Reverend," she purred, running her hands down his chest. "Didn't you know? There *are* no bounds with me."

A line of sweat popped up above his lip, but he didn't budge. Not an inch.

And so, for good measure, she unbuttoned the top button on his shirt and dipped her fingers inside.

Chest hair.

Lord. She loved it.

It was an effort to make herself remember what she was trying to do. She gave a little swivel of her hips that turned out to be shockingly intimate considering his condition. And hers.

If she didn't move on soon, she'd be up in flames.

They'd have to evacuate the sick and the maimed and call the fire department to save the nursing home.

And who will save you, Skylar?

"No bounds at all," she murmured. "Just how close would you like to be, preacher?"

That ought to cool his jets.

And hers.

Time stretched to eternity. He didn't budge. Didn't even flinch.

She tried to read his expression but couldn't. Did the preacher play poker?

When he finally spoke, his voice was deep, husky, sexy.

"Wrong time, wrong place." With his hands on her shoulders, he half picked her up, half scooted her back.

"You're confusing what I do with what I am, Skylar," he said, then turned and walked away.

Good riddance.

Then why did she feel so…bereft?

Chapter Three

From the diary of Anne Beaufort Westmoreland:

September 21, 2001

*T*ranquility Manor. What kind of name is that for a nursing home? Where did they get it anyhow? From that first moon landing? The one where Neil Armstrong radioed Houston and said, "Tranquility Base here. The Apollo mission has landed."

That's what the nursing home feels like. The moon. Cut off from every familiar thing, severed from every loving tie and a long, long way from home. Millions of miles.

With no way to get back.

How am I ever going help bring Michael out of his coma if I don't get out of this horrible negative mood?

Thank goodness for Daniel. He came in this morning earlier than I expected and announced he was staying two weeks. Maybe three.

"What brought this on?" I asked, and he said, "Mom, I haven't had a vacation this year and only a few days off here and there over the last two years. It's high time I took a real vacation."

Well, naturally I'm thrilled to death. Daniel is such a strong, cheerful person. I certainly need that right now, somebody to lean on, at least for a little while.

And maybe Michael does, too. They were always so close. Maybe Daniel will do or say something that will wake his father up, propel him from that bed.

Clarice thinks it's a good thing, too—Daniel staying. She was still at the nursing home when he told me, and she got this cat-eating-cream look that I meant to ask her about, but then the staff started their comings and goings, and I never did get around to asking her why she was looking so smug.

Maybe I'll call her after lunch and ask her. Anyhow, I need to tell her thank you for last night. For the laughter. Lord, the way we carried on you'd think we were teenagers instead of fifty-something matrons with sagging bellies and crow's feet.

I think all that liveliness was good for Michael, too. Once when Clarice was telling one of her wild and funny tales I looked over at Michael and thought I saw his mouth twitch. As if he were trying to say something. Or trying to laugh.

I said to Clarice, "Did you see that?" and she asked, "What?" I said, "Never mind. It was nothing, after all."

Clarice thinks I ought to be getting out more. Going places. Movies, concerts, dinner parties, things like that.

I told her, "No, not yet."

It wouldn't be so much a betrayal of Michael (Lord, knows, he wouldn't want me to do nothing but sit) as a giving up. A loss of hope. An acceptance that life goes on somehow without him.

I won't accept that. Not yet.

Not *ever*. I'm not ever going to act as if my future does not include having Michael by my side. Touching me. Holding me. Loving me.

Chapter Four

Daniel could hear her singing down the hall. *Skylar.* An unusual name for an unusual woman.

Today she wasn't singing bawdy lyrics, though. She was doing some nice, easy blues, the kind Daniel liked to listen to late at night after the neighbors had all turned out their lights and the traffic on the street outside his house had dwindled to an occasional car or two. "In the Wee Small Hours." "Time after Time." "It Only Takes a Moment."

"Someone to Watch Over Me."

Now there was a song that spoke to the heart. And Skylar was singing it with a particular longing that would haunt Daniel for a long time.

He replayed their encounter in the hallway. The sparks he'd felt when he touched her. The excitement. The desire.

Amazing. He'd never experienced anything like it. Was that the thing that had kept his parents' relationship so *alive* all those years? Some kind of electrical charge that passed between them whenever they touched?

Heck, he'd felt the same charge just looking at Skylar.

And then she'd retreated. Not physically. Definitely not physically. But emotionally.

When she'd deliberately baited him with her provocative body language, he'd actually felt her pain. Was that why she'd retreated? Instinct told him that was part of it, and experience told him he was going to do something about it.

He'd never been able to sit still while one of God's creatures was hurting, and so he went to his father's bedside and took his hand.

"Dad, I'm going down the hall a minute." Daniel studied his father closely for any signs that he had heard, but there was nothing. Not even a twitch. "I'll be right back. And I hope to bring a surprise for you."

Following the sound of music, Daniel went down the hall then rounded the corner and came upon the open door. Skylar was standing at the bedside of a thin woman with wispy gray hair, holding her hand and singing in a soft hypnotic voice. She had her back to Daniel.

Unnoticed, he stood in the doorway until the song ended, and then he spoke quietly.

"That was very beautiful."

Skylar jerked as if she'd been shot, then turned slowly toward him.

"It's you." Emotions played over her face. Quick joy, then caution and finally a cool indifference. More than cool. *Cold.*

But Daniel was not deterred. He stepped inside the room saying, "I hope I'm not intruding."

"If I say yes will that stop you?"

"No."

"I thought not." Skylar bent over the woman in the bed, squeezing her hand and smiling. "Mrs. Clements, I want you to meet Daniel Westmoreland. *Reverend* Westmoreland."

"Don't let Skylar's cold shoulder bother you a bit, Reverend. Her bark's worse than her bite."

"Ha!" Skylar bared her teeth and growled in a demonstration that was all bluster. There was not the least bit of animosity in her.

Encouraged, but trying not to take it personally, Daniel smiled at both of them, his gaze lingering on Skylar. She was the most blatantly sensual woman he'd ever seen. The walls seemed closer with her in the room, the air hotter, the humidity higher. So high he could feel his shirt beginning to stick to his skin in wet patches.

If he stopped to ponder, he'd probably discover motives he'd rather not think about. Best not to think. Best to go forward on the assumption that he was here with laudable intentions and a pure heart.

"After you've finished here, I wonder if you'd join me for a cup of coffee?"

"Why?"

Her blunt question took him aback. If he'd opened his mouth he'd have sputtered like a schoolboy. Instead he did what his father had always taught him. *Never speak before your brain is totally engaged, Daniel. You can avoid lots of hot spots that way.*

Skylar leaned slightly forward, and her sweater stretched tightly over her breasts, making it perfectly clear she was not wearing a bra.

Daniel was certain the gesture was deliberate. If she thought she was going to send him running with those tactics, she was sorely mistaken. In the course of his ministry he'd seen worse. More than one distraught wife on the brink of divorce had tried to entice him to offer more than sage advice. But he'd never seen the ploy used more effectively.

Though surely Skylar Tate had something more in mind for him than enticement. Being burned at the stake was more like it. And she was lighting the fire.

"We got off on the wrong foot, and I'd like to change that. Also, there's another matter I'd like to discuss with you."

"A…I don't drink coffee. B…you can state your piece right here. I have no secrets from Harriet."

"Shoo." Harriet made a waving motion with her hand. "Go on out of here. I'm going to rest now." With that, she closed her eyes.

"I'm not finished. There's another song I want to sing for you. Your favorite."

Though her mouth twitched as if she were suppressing a grin, Harriet kept her eyes shut.

"Harriet…" Skylar leaned over and smoothed back the old woman's hair. "Don't do this to me."

The indomitable Harriet lay still as a turtle on a log. Sighing, Skylar grabbed her purse and flounced out the door. Daniel followed.

She sped up, keeping two paces ahead of him. Deliberately. Long angry strides. Provocative sway of hips.

Increasing his pace, he drew alongside her and matched her stride for stride.

"You don't have to do this, you know."

"Do what?" She glanced at him, her eyes shooting blue fire.

"Run from me."

"Are all preachers this arrogant, or is it just you?"

"Determined."

"Pigheaded."

"Sometimes." That made her smile. "Especially when I've made a complete jackass of myself twice with you already."

Her smile got bigger. "I didn't know preachers used words like that."

"I'm a man, not a profession."

"Okay. I deserved that."

She ran her hands through her long hair, tossing it back from her forehead. Daniel felt gut-punched. He was not seeing Skylar in the nursing home wearing a yellow sweater, but Skylar in his bedroom with a tiny bit of sequins decorating her breasts.

"Just because I want people to judge me by what I do, that doesn't mean everybody wants the same thing," she said.

Because of what Clarice had told him, Daniel could make several good guesses about her motives, but he didn't pause to ask why? He would save that for later. Besides, she probably wouldn't tell him.

"So…" She glanced sideways at him, then quickly looked away. "Tell me about your bouts of jackassery."

"The first time was yesterday when I stood tongue-tied in the hallway while you passed right by me, and the second was my ignominious retreat this morning."

Her laughter was big and hearty. Refreshing.

"I never once heard my daddy admit to being a jackass, though he was. The world's biggest."

"Tell me about your father."

"He's dead." She stared straight ahead.

"I'm sorry."

"I don't want your sympathy. I don't *need* it."

"What do you need, Skylar?"

She whirled on him, hands on hips, eyes blazing. "Don't you *dare* patronize me. Ever."

"I didn't mean to be patronizing. I was…"

"Being a *preacher*." She marched ahead of him, but he caught up in two easy strides. She shot him an angry look. "Don't ask questions, don't get sanctimonious and don't get too close. Is that clear?"

"Yes." Clearer than she knew.

Here was a woman on the run from a past she found unbearable. Daniel wanted to reach out to her with compassion, just as he reached out to his flock in Atlanta.

Then why didn't he? What was holding him back?

A sideways glance at Skylar followed by the quickening of his pulse gave him the answer. His interest in her was more than professional—far, far more.

As they walked along in uneasy silence, Daniel struggled with temptation.

You're a long way from Atlanta, Daniel.

I know.

You could have a fling with her. Who would ever know?

I would.

He tried to think of something to say to her, anything to take his mind off the conversation that was playing in his head. Desperate, he latched on to the first thing that came into his mind.

"The weather's beautiful today, isn't it?"

"Yes, I love this time of year."

"So do I."

It wasn't brilliant repartee, but it did the trick. His pulse was almost back to normal.

"Did you ever race outside naked and scrunch on the leaves?" she said.

So much for normal pulse rates.

"I can't say that I ever have."

"You should. It might loosen you up a bit."

"Do you think I need loosening up?"

"Yes." She laughed. "You act as if I'm going to bite you."

"I'm not so sure that you won't."

"You aren't?"

"No. I've heard you growl. Remember?"

"You're not so bad for a..."

"Don't say it."

"Okay. I won't."

They rounded the corner and when Daniel touched her elbow to guide her into the lounge, the sexual currents between them were so strong he felt burned. He immediately broke contact. Skylar glanced at him, but thankfully didn't comment.

Daniel hurried to the coffeemaker and poured two cups. "How do you like yours?" he asked.

"Hot."

Was she baiting him? Toying with him? Steeling himself against further assault, Daniel set the two cups on the table then pulled out a chair for Skylar.

"Are you always such a gentleman?"

"No."

"Good."

What did she mean by that? That she wanted to see him in a situation where he was being less than well-bred? In bed, for instance?

She leaned one elbow on the table and propped her chin in a cupped hand, smiling that little devil's grin of hers. "You're different from most men."

He wanted to ask if she meant that as a compliment, but he didn't dare. After all, his interest in her wasn't personal. *Yeah, and cats don't have climbing gears.*

"I suppose you're wondering why I wanted to speak with you privately."

"Not really. Don't all men want the same thing?"

Refusing to be baited once more, Daniel leaned back in his chair, sipping coffee and studying Skylar. She remained perfectly still, chin cupped, staring at him with eyes so wide they reminded him of pieces of early night sky just after the rising of a full harvest moon. Dark, dark blue. Soft and velvety looking. Full of beauty and endless mystery.

Never taking his eyes off hers, Daniel set his cup on the table.

"I want you to sing for my father, Skylar."

Her elbow slipped a little, but she recovered quickly.

"Why? You don't approve of me and you certainly don't like me."

"To answer your question...because your singing is beautiful, and I think it will help him. And now I have one of my own. How did you come to those ridiculous and false conclusions?"

"They're false?"

"Yes."

"You like me?"

"Very much."

"And you *approve* of me?"

"Yes. Unequivocally."

She sat upright and gripped her coffee cup. "My God...why?"

"You have such a wonderful spirit, Skylar, such liveliness. How could anyone not approve of you?"

"My fa—" She bit her lower lip, then took a sip of coffee before setting her cup on the table. "That's not a very preacherly answer."

"I guess I'm not a very preacherly person." He smiled at her.

"Good. I'll sing for your father."

Her hand looked very small resting on the table between

them. Soft. Fragile looking. He wanted to touch it, but resisted.

"I'm glad, Skylar." He smiled again.

"But that's all I'll do for you."

"I'm afraid I don't follow you."

"I won't linger in your father's room for chats. I won't come down here to the lounge to share a cup of coffee. I won't talk about myself, period. And I certainly won't give you a chance to convert me."

"Convert you?"

"Yes. To *save* me." She stood up, and every bit of her was on full, glorious display. "Women like me are a preacher's greatest challenge, Daniel. I won't be yours."

He pushed his chair back and stood up, his movements slow and deliberate. His face a mask.

Skylar experienced a moment of panic. Had she gone too far this time? He took a step closer, his eyes blazing.

She'd been wrong about his face being a mask. He had the determined, fiery look of a hunter closing in on his quarry.

He caught her upper arm, his movements smooth and quick. Unexpected. His face...

Lord, he had the face of a man bent on kissing.

"What you are going to do?" she asked.

"Escort you to my father's room. You said you'd sing."

"I didn't say right this very minute."

"Is this not a good time for you?"

She'd planned to stay at the nursing home all morning. If she said no, she'd have to leave. Just on general principles. And if she left she'd have nothing to do but rattle around in her parents' house with nothing for company except a sometimes surly cat and all those memories.

"Well, yes. It's fine. Okay. I'll sing."

"Good."

He led her to the door and down the hall, still holding on to her arm. And it felt good. So good she didn't tell him to let her go.

She simply wasn't going to think about that right now. She was going to concentrate on the job at hand. And singing for the patients at Tranquility Manor was a job for her, one she dearly loved. No pay, of course. Not in the traditional manner. But the sense of satisfaction was enormous.

There was Harriet who patted Skylar's hand and told her she didn't know how she'd get through her days without those songs. And there was dear little Mrs. Lyons whose first name she didn't even know, a retired schoolteacher who still got up every morning and dressed as if she were headed to Vicksburg High to teach algebra and trigonometry. She always requested hymns, and while Skylar sang Mrs. Lyons leaned back with her eyes closed and her hands crossed over her flat breasts as if she were praying. Then afterward, she'd hand Skylar a single flower, usually one of the African violets she grew under lights, sometimes a rose she'd stolen from the gardens on the grounds of the manor.

Denton Lovett always requested honky-tonk songs, then sat in his chair laughing till tears rolled down his cheeks, while his roommate, Mr. Crimpton, turned his face to the window and pretended not to be listening. But once Skylar had seen him cup his hand around his ear so he could hear better.

She loved coming here. Meeting the people. Singing to them. Making them smile.

But she'd stop coming in a New York minute if she thought Daniel Westmoreland had any ideas of worming his way into her life. She was satisfied with things exactly the way they were, thank you very much.

Or was she?

"Here we are," Daniel said, and she realized thankfully they'd finally reached their destination.

Still he held onto her arm. And still she let him.

She didn't know why. Didn't want to know why.

"Dad, I've brought someone to meet you. Her name is Skylar Tate, and she has the most beautiful voice this side of heaven. She's going to sing for you."

He squeezed her arm. Whether it was a conscious gesture she didn't know. But it felt good. Oh, it felt so good. Intimate somehow. As if the two of them were sharing a beautiful private moment. Some lovely secret.

She wasn't going to think about that either. About why she felt a sense of longing. Why she felt as if she were melting inside. Melting. *Melting.*

"Skylar, this is Michael, the world's best dad and a world-class high-altitude filmmaker. He loves music of all kinds, but most of all he loves the blues."

"So do I."

Daniel finally released her and stepped back. But not too far. She could feel his solid presence just behind her, slightly to the left. Body heat. Delicious currents. Sexual charges in small voltages, big enough to sizzle but not ignite.

Not yet.

Now where had that thought come from? She'd have to pay attention here. She'd have to keep her mind on her business.

"Michael." She spoke his name softly.

The sight of him moved her to compassion. She leaned over the bed, touched his sunken cheek, smoothed his hair back from his forehead. His skin felt dry and papery. The skin of a man no longer inhabiting his body. The skin of a virile outdoorsman who had been too long in the bed.

Was his spirit still intact? Was it somewhere just beneath the layers of deep sleep waiting to be awakened?

And could she do it with her music?

Skylar felt an awesome sense of responsibility and hard on its heels a sort of panic. Is that what Daniel expected of her? Miracles?

She couldn't deliver. She needed to drag him from the room and explain that to him. She needed to say, *I can't do this. I can't be your last hope.*

That was silly, of course. He was a man of the cloth who depended on a much higher power than she.

He wanted her to sing. That was all.

"I'm going to sing an old, old song from the thirties. It's one of my favorites. I guess it's more properly called a torch song, but still it has that nice bluesy feel. Especially the way Bette Midler sings it."

Without further preamble Skylar started singing "The Glory of Love." Putting her heart into it. Her soul.

And when it was over the room was so quiet she could hear the beating of her own heart.

And Daniel's. He'd moved in close enough to touch.

She turned to him, her heart hammering, her cheeks damp.

Slowly he reached up and touched her tears. Wiped them tenderly with the pads of his fingers.

"You're crying."

"I always cry when I sing the blues."

Chapter Five

I hear singing. Is it angels? Am I dead?

I can't be dead. I have places to go, promises to keep. To Anne. Beautiful, beautiful Anne.

Where are you, Anne? I can't feel you. Are you there? Talk to me, my beloved.

There's so much fog, so much distance. I can't reach you. I can't touch you.

I want to. I'm trying.

I'm trying so hard. So hard.

My eyes...heavy...fog...everywhere.

I...can't...hold...on.

Anne...Annie...

Chapter Six

There are hundreds of ways a man can touch a woman. Perhaps even thousands.

And in that moment, with time suspended and Skylar's tears fresh on his fingertips, Daniel knew them all. And longed.

What he saw in her shining eyes was a genuine, bone-deep goodness that she couldn't hide no matter how hard she tried. He saw the kindness of her heart and the generosity of her soul. He saw her fierce will and indomitable spirit. He saw a giving person who had been treated carelessly.

And his heart lifted in spontaneous prayer. *Father, don't ever let me treat this woman carelessly.*

Cupping her face as tenderly as if she were a moonbeam, Daniel bent down and kissed her on the cheek. Softly. Briefly.

When he stepped back she flushed the color of a rose, then busied herself patting the covers on Michael's bed.

"As much as I love singing, I don't want to tire you with a lengthy concert the first day. Tomorrow I'll bring my guitar, and, if you're up to it, I'll sing two or three songs."

She glanced over her shoulder at Daniel, then quickly away. He'd never seen her nervous. Should he apologize?

No. That would call attention to her obvious discomfort, and no woman wants to be put in that position. He'd learned that the hard way growing up with two sisters.

Especially Hannah. Lord have mercy, one time with her was enough to teach any man a lesson. She'd lost a foot-race to him after swearing she could beat any boy in Vicksburg, and when he'd called attention to her chagrin she'd socked him in the stomach so hard he'd lost his breath.

"Don't you dare ever make a woman feel uncomfortable again, Daniel Westmoreland," she'd said.

"Yes, ma'am," he'd said, although she was only ten years old at the time and a long way from womanhood.

He couldn't say the same for Skylar. She was all woman and then some.

And she was getting ready to walk out of the room.

"Thank you for coming here, Skylar. It means a lot to…"

If he said *my father,* he'd be telling a lie. Michael didn't seem to know he was in the world. And if he said *my family,* that would be another falsehood, because he was the only one in his family who knew.

And so he told the barefaced truth. "It means a lot to me," he said.

"Will you be here tomorrow?"

"Yes."

"What time?"

"Morning, probably. Mom still tries to spend every night here with Dad."

"In that case, I'll come in the afternoon."

In order to avoid him? He didn't ask. Maybe she was arranging her time that way so she could give his mother something to hold on to. Something new. Music, and the possibility of a miracle.

"That will be great."

He'd bring plenty of books tomorrow. Enough to last him into the afternoon. He hadn't spent that much time with his mother, and she needed his company. Didn't she?

"Are you headed home?" he asked and she nodded. "I'll walk you to the car," he added.

"That's not necessary."

"I insist."

He didn't take her arm. No need to push his luck. From the way she was striding down the hall, he was courting danger if not outright disaster. All in all, it would be best to content himself just to be in the same vicinity as Skylar Tate.

When Daniel pushed open the heavy front doors, the janitor waved at them.

"'Bye, Miss Skylar. Will we see you again tomorrow?"

"If the sun shines and the creek doesn't rise, Mr. Clements."

Bob slapped his knee and hooted. "Lord, Preacher, you got a live one there."

"He doesn't have me at all, Bob. I'm just tolerating his company." She gave Daniel an arch look. "For the moment."

He held the door for her and caught a whiff of her fragrance as she passed through. It was erotic. Designed to give a man all kinds of fantasies.

"I'll have to remember to mind my p's and q's."

"See that you do that."

"Which way?"

"Beyond the pond."

"The T-Bird, right?"

"How did you know?"

Her car was a red Thunderbird convertible, not old enough to be an antique but too old to be called merely used. He could have said, *Because it has flash and style and because it's out of the ordinary.*

"It suits you," he said, instead, then opened her door and tried not to stare at her legs when she climbed inside.

She hung her left hand casually over the door frame, and he could see a chip in the polish on her ring finger. He had a sudden, intense urge to bend down and kiss that tiny imperfection.

He shifted his gaze from her hand to her face, and found himself falling into the enormous blue expanse of her shining eyes. The long, deep look stretched to eternity, and when it curved around and came back to the present, Daniel was short of breath.

And sweating, besides.

"Skylar..."

She downshifted. "Goodbye, Reverend," she said, and her car shot forward, leaving him in the hot, boiling sun of a September day that was parading around as summer.

He stuck his hands in his pockets and walked back to the nursing home, whistling.

The song was "The Glory of Love."

The message light was blinking when Skylar got home, but she ignored it, climbed into the shower and stayed so long the soft white skin on her fingers and toes began to pucker. As if she could wash away her sins. As if she could wash away the seeds of hope that had sprung to life at the nursing home when Daniel kissed her cheek.

"Bull," she scoffed. And then when that wasn't enough, she beat the shower walls with her palms and said, "Hellfire and damnation."

Then she turned her face up to the water and waited to feel like herself again, that sassy don't-give-a-damn self who spit in the eye of the world, that carefree woman who scoffed at convention and broke rules and dared anybody to clip her wings, that independent woman who guarded her hard-won peace with fierce resolve.

She didn't want tenderness. She didn't need gentleness. She didn't crave the hands of a good man on her cheek making her feel as if she'd just been crowned princess of the universe.

Did she?

Skylar jerked a towel off the rack and stood on the bathroom floor dripping while Pussy Willow rubbed her arched back against the door frame.

"I just won't go to the nursing home tomorrow. That's all."

Her cat purred her approval, then meowed once and headed to the kitchen in her dainty, mincing gait.

"You're hungry, are you?"

Skylar poured cat food into Pussy Willow's blue china dish, then fixed herself a big roast beef sandwich and ate the whole thing, all the while casting a baleful eye toward the blinking red light announcing that she had voice mail and that quite possibly it was urgent.

Finally Skylar gave in. She had a fleeting thought that it might be Daniel before a familiar voice filled her kitchen.

"Hi, Skylar, this is Pete down at Babe's. I heard you were back in town and just wanted to invite you to come on down here and sing for us. For the forty-'leventh time. Say yes, Sky.''

Pete Sanford was an old buddy of Skylar's from the early days of the band. A former linebacker with the Saints, he'd taken up music when an injury had forced his retirement. He'd played lead guitar with the New Blues for a year, then decided life on the road wasn't for him.

He'd returned to his hometown of Vicksburg, married his high-school sweetheart, then bought a nightclub and adopted five children, in that order.

He was big, brash and lovable. A hard man to tell no to.

Every year when he asked her to sing in his club, that's what Skylar had told him.

She picked up the phone and dialed his number.

''Pete...when do you want me to sing?''

After she'd hung up the receiver, she stood in the middle of her kitchen with her hands on her hips still waiting to feel like herself.

The nightclub's sign was blue and pink neon, the kind some people called gaudy. To Skylar it was lively and festive, and maybe that's because she knew the owner of Babe's, knew him to be a big-hearted, fun-loving man who looked like an oversize gorilla but who wouldn't hurt a fly.

Pete was waiting for her. He pulled her into a bear hug then leaned back and said, ''Let me look at you...my God, you're more gorgeous than I remember.''

Cupping his mouth he yelled, ''Steffie, come see who I've got in here.''

His wife came at a fast trot, her cheeks bright pink and her wild red hair held back from her lovely face with two red combs.

''My goodness, Skylar!'' She hugged her hard. ''We

haven't seen you since Christmas three years ago. Shame on you for staying away so long.''

"Well, I'm back now. How're the children?''

"They're a handful. Just like Pete.''

"They act like their mom. Every one of them with a temper as wild as her red hair,'' Pete responded.

Skylar loved the lively give-and-take between Pete and his wife. Envied it, really. Why couldn't she have what they did? A good marriage, kids to love, a real home?

She knew the answer to that, of course. She didn't have any of those things because she didn't know whether they would work for her and she was afraid to find out.

Or maybe she didn't have them because she was too darned ornery and unconventional and…well, just plain *wild*.

"But enough about us,'' Pete said. "Come on, Skylar. I'll introduce you to the band, give you a chance to run through some things with them.'' He hugged her. "Gosh, I can't tell you how much this means to me, Sky. I've been wanting you here for years. What made you change your mind?''

Skylar could have told him any number of things: that she didn't like sitting around nights doing nothing, that she liked to keep in practice during the band's off-season, that she loved singing anywhere, anytime.

Instead she looked into the sweet trusting face of her old friend who had been with the band during the lean years, the years when they'd all pile into the old 1950s school bus they'd painted a psychedelic blue and go out for burgers after a performance because that was as far as their money would stretch.

"I changed my mind because I've met a man who makes me know just how lonely my life is, Pete.''

Pete didn't ask what was holding her back. He knew. Instead he gave her another bear hug.

"Anything I can do to help, Sky? You know Steffie and I would do anything in the world for you."

She squeezed his hand, then reached for Steffie's.

"Just let me sing and feed me a burger...for old time's sake."

"You got it, kid."

Chapter Seven

From the diary of Anne Beaufort Westmoreland:

September 22, 2001

Tragedy comes so quickly. How can this be?

Last night as I lay in bed beside Michael I could swear I heard him whisper my name. "Annie," he said, just like that. Once and then no more.

I was holding him close, stroking his back the way he's always loved and telling him how much I love him. "Michael," I told him, "I adore you, I love you more than life itself, you are my whole universe, my darling. Please, please come back to me. *Please*, Michael."

That's when he said my name. No more than a breath, really. A sigh. Or was it a dream? Was it just the force of my own desire that gave him voice?

Whatever it was, it gave me hope. I woke up this morning with a bounce in my step. The first thing I did after I got out of bed, after I'd kissed my husband and said, "Good morning, my beloved," was fling open the blinds to let the sunshine in.

And that's when I saw that something wasn't right with Michael. Other than the coma, I mean.

Panicked, I raced into the hall still in my gown, screaming for a nurse.

Why I didn't use the call button is beyond me. No, it isn't. Not really. I've always been one to give voice to my pain. I did it when I got the phone call saying Michael had been caught in an avalanche in the Himalayas.

And that's how I did it this morning when I saw the first outward signs of pneumonia. Not that I knew what it was. Not then. But later. After the doctor had arrived. After the poking and prodding, the X-rays to confirm.

"It's pneumonia, Anne. Definitely in the left lung, and I don't like the looks of the right one," the doctor told me.

By then I'd somehow managed to get enough control to ask intelligent questions.

"How serious is that?"

"I won't lie. Michael's been bedridden for four months. He's not in top-notch condition, and he's immobile. It's very serious, Anne."

"Is he going to die?"

How I asked that question without screaming is a mystery to me. I guess we're all given enough strength for the moment. That's what Daniel says.

He's down the hall calling Emily and Hannah. There's a phone in the room, but still, we don't want Michael to hear. We don't want him to know that there's a chance he might die.

That's what the doctor told me. "I won't lie to you, Anne," he said. "Pneumonia could kill Michael, but we're going to do everything in our power to see that it doesn't."

Thank God, Daniel is here. I'm sure Emily will be here sometime this afternoon, though I told Daniel to tell both girls it's not necessary that they come. Not yet, at least.

Emily will come, though. It will only take her a few hours to drive down.

I'm not sure about Hannah. I know she'll want to come. I think she's winding up an assignment, and if that's the case she'll probably fly in tomorrow.

Clarice is already here.

God, what would I do without my friends? She came bearing goodies, mostly chocolate. She said, "I'm here for the duration, and I'm here to see that you don't starve."

Isn't that just like her to stave off hunger with a pound of chocolate-covered almonds, a pound of chocolate-covered peanuts and a twelve-pack of milk-chocolate candy bars.

Also, isn't that just like her to make me laugh in the midst of tears?

I thought I heard Linda and Jane out in the hall a while ago. Naturally Clarice called them. She believes in rallying the friends.

I do, too, though I told her and Daniel that I need some time alone with Michael. They understood.

Here's the thing. No matter how much you love your family and your friends, the relationship that will always come first is the one with your true love.

It's quiet in the hall now. I can almost believe that

I'm back at Belle Rose with Michael, that he's just walked into the room and hugged me from behind, that he's leading me to the bed with that sweet, sweet smile on his face and that special look of love in his eyes.

That he's going to lie down with me and hold me close and whisper, "Don't let go, Annie. Don't ever let go."

And I won't, my darling. I promise.

I *won't*.

I'm going to lie beside him now. I'm going to wrap my arms around his fever-hot body and lie so close I can synchronize our breathing, our heartbeats. Then I'll will all my strength into him. I'll smooth back his hair and kiss his lips and whisper, "Don't let go, Michael. As long as you don't let go, you'll be all right. As long as you hold onto me, we'll always be together."

I love you. I love you, Michael.

Chapter Eight

I feel you, Anne. I feel your body next to mine.

Tears? Is that tears?

Don't cry, my precious. I'm not going to leave you. We have too much loving ahead of us, too much laughter.

Keep talking to me, angel. I need the sound of your voice. It grounds me, pulls me back from whatever is at the other end of the tunnel.

Yes…that's it. Keep talking. Ah, yes. And your hands. Such a soft and tender touch.

There. Over my heart. I feel the imprint of your warm hand.

Don't let go.

I love you, too, Annie. I love you.

Chapter Nine

On the off chance that Daniel would have gone home, Skylar waited until afternoon to go to Tranquility Manor. But still, she scanned the parking lot. Half hoping.

And there was his car. Georgia license plates. For some foolish reason her heart lifted and her step was light as she walked through the front doors of the nursing home.

Bob Clements saw her coming, and stepped out of the janitorial supply room to greet her.

"You're late coming today. Harriet's been askin' 'bout you."

"I worked last night. At Pete's club down by the river. I hope Harriet didn't worry."

"A little bit. You know how she is."

"I'll go see her...right after I stop by Michael Westmoreland's room."

She had to go there first. She had to know if Daniel was in the nursing home.

Bob shook his head. "Lordy, lordy, that family's got a heap of trouble today."

Skylar went pale. "What happened?"

"That poor man's done gone and took the pneumonia. I've seen lots of folk leave here feet first when that happens."

"Thanks for telling me, Bob."

Walk down the hall, she told herself. *Don't run. Make it look natural. You're just stopping by to check on one of your patients.*

That's how she viewed all the people in the nursing home. As *her* patients. After all, music was the best medicine. Right after laughter. Maybe even before.

As she neared Michael Westmoreland's room she could hear the murmur of voices. Daniel's voice. Deep. Rich. Sending shivers all over her. Speeding up her heartbeat.

She paused outside the door with her hand over her chest. Really, she shouldn't go in there. The Westmorelands were in the midst of a family crisis. They didn't need her.

Probably didn't want her. She'd just be in the way.

Besides, she wanted to avoid Daniel, didn't she? Wasn't that her whole purpose for arriving late today?

Skylar lifted her chin at a determined angle, and strode on down the hall.

Daniel was in the midst of responding to something Emily had said when he felt a tug on his heartstrings that was akin to a sharp pain.

Skylar.

"Excuse me, Em." He headed to the door.

"Daniel, what's wrong?"

"Nothing. I'll be right back."

He flung open the door and saw her disappearing down the hallway.

"Skylar...wait." She turned when she heard him. Thank God, she turned and waited.

He caught up to her and touched her arm, then drowned. That's the only way he could describe the sensation that overtook him. Total immersion. Loss of breath. Focus on one thing. Skylar's eyes.

"I heard about your father, Daniel. I'm sorry."

"Thank you. You weren't going to stop to say hello?"

"I didn't want to intrude."

"You could never be an intrusion. More like a welcome breath of spring."

"The rest of your family might not share that opinion. Especially today."

"No. They'd be glad to see you. Besides, I'd like you to meet my mother."

"Daniel...don't."

"I didn't mean that the way it sounded, Skylar. I'd like you to meet her for her sake. Right now she can use all the support she can get."

He loved watching the play of emotions over Skylar's face. It was like sitting on a porch swing on a partly cloudy day watching the sky change from a sun-suffused blue to a portentous gray, then back again.

Finally she'd settled the matter in her own mind. When she stepped back from him, Daniel realized how close he'd been standing. Close enough to smell the fragrance she wore.

Did she put it in the crook of her elbows? In that soft spot where the blue veins pulsed? Did she spray it behind her knees so that when she walked she left a siren's trail?

Was that what had called him from his father's room? The scent of a siren?

Or had it been something more?

His heart. Yearning.

"I'll see your father again sometime soon, Daniel. I want you to know this about me: I don't abandon my patients. Once I start singing for one of them, I don't give up. I don't walk away."

"I didn't think you would."

"They count on me. Whether they can say so or not, I know they do."

"I believe my father does. He looked and seemed more peaceful after you'd sung to him."

"Thank you for telling me that."

Daniel had to touch her. He *had* to. And so he held out his hand, and she took it.

"Thank *you*, Skylar. I hope someday my dad can thank you in person."

"Oh, he will, Daniel...if I'm still around."

Daniel couldn't take that personally. After all Skylar Tate was a busy woman. A professional singer. Almost famous.

"I should go back," he said, then he released her and watched her walk away, watched her until she'd rounded the corner and he could no longer see the vivid blue sweater that matched her eyes.

The scent of her perfume lingered, and Daniel inhaled deeply. A man could get drunk on a woman like her. A man could lose his sense completely.

If he weren't careful.

And Daniel wanted to be careful. Didn't he?

The brief euphoria he'd felt in Skylar's presence stayed with him all the way down the hall. But the minute he stepped into his father's room, it vanished.

Everybody turned toward him. Expectant. Hopeful.

His mother. His baby sister. His mother's three best friends.

Say something to make us feel better, Daniel, they silently pleaded. *Tell us everything's going to be all right.*

"Any change?" he asked.

"None," Clarice said. "The doctor was in here while you were gone. The right lung's still clear. Thank God."

Maybe he should. If he were the minister he ought to be, Daniel would lead them all in a prayer of thanksgiving for that small sign.

He couldn't remember the last time he'd had a real conversation with God. He couldn't remember the last time he'd fallen to his knees and felt the power of an all-loving Father descend on him.

His skin felt hot and his mouth dry. Like a man with a fever. A man with a soul sickness.

What was happening to him? And what was he going to do about it?

Emily, who had been standing with her arm around Anne, left her mother's side and bent over Michael.

"Daddy, you have to get well. My wedding's less than two weeks away, and I want you to give me away." Tears leaked from the corners of her eyes and rolled down her cheeks. "I've always counted on you to do that, Daddy."

Anne's chin went up as she stationed herself by her husband's bed and began to massage his feet.

"Of *course,* he's going to do that. Michael's just resting up for the big occasion, aren't you, darling?" She glared at everybody in the room, her eyes blazing. "I won't hear any more gloom-and-doom talk in here. Clarice, you and Linda and Jane take Emily somewhere and feed her dinner. She hasn't had a bite to eat since she got here."

"What about you, Anne? You need to eat, too. Come with us," pleaded Jane.

Anne just gave her that look, and Clarice grabbed Jane's arm and practically dragged her toward the door.

"Anne's got enough chocolate to see her through the

siege of Vicksburg. Come on. Let's give Michael a chance to rest."

"Are you coming, Daniel?" Emily asked.

"Not yet. I'll grab a bite later."

His mother waited until the door had closed behind them.

"I'm fine here, Daniel. You should have gone with them."

"I'll get something later, Mom."

"What's this all about, Daniel?"

"Nothing."

He hoped he was telling the truth. He hoped his strange malaise of spirit was a passing thing. An insignificant blip on his life's screen that was of no consequence.

"You haven't seemed yourself these last couple of days."

"I have a lot on my mind. We all do."

"Yes, that's true."

It was getting dark outside. Daniel went to the window to lower the blinds.

"No...leave them. It's going to be clear tonight. Maybe we can see the stars."

We. The two of them together. His mother and his father. Lying side by side in the bed watching the evening show as if it were staged exclusively for them.

And that's the way it should be. If there was any justice at all.

If there was a God.

Agony ripped through Daniel. He had to get out. He had to leave the room. He had to leave the nursing home with its awful collection of frail, needy humanity.

"Will you be all right here tonight?"

"Yes."

"You're sure? I'll stay if you need me."

"I know you will. But Michael and I need to be alone."

"You'll call me if you need me?"

"Yes."

Not at home, though. Not at Belle Rose. Daniel couldn't bear to go back to that big empty house with no one except Emily to keep him company. Besides, Jake was flying in tonight. The two of them would want to be together without him.

Pairs. The world was made up of pairs.

Noah's ark. All the animals going in two by two.

Daniel felt an insane urge to laugh, then wondered if he might be going crazy.

"You have my cell phone number?" he asked.

"Yes. Now shoo, go on, get out of here."

"Good night, Mom."

He kissed Anne's cheek, then she nodded toward the bed. Dutifully Daniel leaned down to bid his father good-night.

Michael's face felt too hot. Like a man who had gathered memorabilia from thirty-something years of marriage then lit a big bonfire inside himself and was standing back watching it all burn. Like a man trying to say goodbye.

"Good night, Dad," Daniel said, and then he pleaded silently, *Don't leave us, Dad. Not yet. Please. There's too much I need to ask you.*

Chapter Ten

Babe's had always been a popular nightspot for Vicksburg's revelers and music lovers, but never more than when Skylar Tate started singing there. Word had spread quickly around town that the lead singer for the New Blues was appearing in Pete Sanford's club down by the river. The star of the hottest video on the market.

By eight o'clock there was standing room only. By nine there was such a crowd of people standing that the waitresses could hardly find their way through to deliver the drinks. In spite of the rain. In spite of the biggest downpour Vicksburg had seen in a long time.

That's why, when Skylar took the stage and gazed out over the crowd she missed him. That's why she was well into her second set, the one that featured ''Someone to Watch Over Me,'' the one where the crowd became hushed and attentive, before she saw Daniel Westmoreland. Perched on a stool at the end of the bar. Nursing a drink.

She nearly lost control of the song. Mark on the keyboard gave her a funny look, and she winked at him to show that she knew exactly what she was doing. That the long pause was a new twist on the arrangement.

She finished the Gershwin tune and segued into another love ballad. But her mind was only half on "Try a Little Tenderness." Instead it was on the man at the bar. The drop-dead gorgeous preacher who couldn't have shocked her more if she'd seen him down on the riverboats placing wads of money on the table and trying to put the right spin on a pair of dice.

Why was he at Babe's?

It was none of her business, of course. Except that Michael was one of her patients now, and naturally she was concerned that something might have happened to him, so wasn't it logical that she should talk to Daniel as soon as her set was over?

Daniel had thought to outrun his demons, but there they were, still sitting on his shoulders sneering while he downed one drink after another. Downed his drinks and listened to Skylar Tate singing. What huge irony. Run from demons and discover an angel.

He hadn't been looking for her when he came to the nightclub, hadn't even known she was working here. But who could miss her car?

In fact, he hadn't planned anything. After he'd left the nursing home he'd driven around and ended up here, searching for answers and finding Skylar Tate, dressed in a sequined gown that showed every curve of her body as well as an enticing glimpse of leg.

He recognized the song she was singing. It was the same one she'd sung for his father. And she was looking his way.

Had she spotted him through the smoke and the crowd?

He lifted his glass to her, viewed her briefly through the amber liquid, then finished the drink. His fourth? His fifth? He'd lost count.

As soon as her last song ended, Skylar made her way toward the bar. She had never gone into the crowd after a set, and now she knew why. Hands were all over her, reaching, grabbing, touching. Catcalls. "Whoa, baby, come on over here." "Come to papa, dollface." "If you're looking for me, here I am."

It was a good thing it was Pete's night off, or heads would roll. He was fiercely protective of her.

Not that she needed protecting. Skylar could take care of herself, and preferred it that way.

Yeah, and elephants can fly.

Daniel was sitting slightly to the left, and even from a distance she could tell he'd had too much to drink. What was she going to do when she got to the bar? Tell him to leave? Act like a mother hen?

She didn't know. She'd just have to play it by ear. Hadn't she always? Given a choice between planning ahead and spontaneity, she'd chose the latter every time.

The man sitting next to Daniel left, and Skylar slid onto the barstool.

"Hello, Daniel."

"Skylar."

He lifted his glass to her. His words were already slurring. He was worse off than she'd thought.

"Has something happened to your dad?" Surely not. Surely he wouldn't be here.

"No. He's the same."

Skylar breathed a little sigh of relief.

"You're a little out of your element here, aren't you?"

"Why?"

"Preachers don't go to bars."

"How do you know? Did you take a poll?"

"No, but I can spot them a mile away. Built-in radar."

"Your radar needs a checkup. I'm not a preacher."

"Since when?"

"Don't know. A long, long time."

So that was it. Daniel was in the throes of doubt and self-examination, probably self-recrimination as well. Skylar had been on that slippery slope many times, and she knew what a lonely and dangerous place it was.

The smart thing to do would be to walk away and leave Daniel to his own devices. He was a strong man, both physically and emotionally. You didn't have to be a genius to figure that out.

But then, you didn't have to be a genius to know that she'd never been one to resist fallen angels. And the harder they fell, the more appeal they had for her.

"You have a lot on your mind," she said.

"'Pears that way."

"Why don't you let me call you a cab so you can go home and do your thinking where it's quiet and peaceful?"

"No. I can't go home."

"Why not?"

"Lots of reasons. Too many to name."

Out of the corner of her eye she saw the band file back into place. It was almost time for her last set.

Walk away. Don't get involved.

"I have to go back on stage. Don't go anywhere. I'll be back."

Lord, had she come back to Mississippi and grown a conscience? At this late date?

"I'm not leaving. I have nowhere left to go."

His words haunted her, followed her all the way to the stage. She walked to the center and began to sing.

* * *

Skylar was singing the blues, the most evocative songs on the face of the earth. And perhaps the truest. The music stripped away what few inhibitions Daniel had left, stripped off his hide and left nothing behind but a puff of breath and a beating heart. Just the essentials.

And the memories…

He was six years old, standing by the riverbank with his first fish and the certainty that he owned the world. He was ten and racing down the hill in front of Belle Rose with his hands above his head, letting the bike chart its own course. He was fifteen and in lust with Martha Graham who sat in front of him in algebra class and didn't know pi from a hole in the ground but had the cutest backside he'd ever seen. He was twenty-three and knew all the answers to the great cosmic questions.

He was thirty-one and didn't know anything. He was thirty-one and standing in the parking lot of the nursing home with his face lifted to the rain shouting, ''Where are you God? Can you see me down here? Can you hear me? Have you moved off and left me?''

There was no answer. Or maybe he wasn't listening any more. Maybe he was the one who had moved away.

He was thirty-one and sitting in a bar looking for anesthesia.

When the last set ended, the lights dimmed and the crowd drifted back home. Skylar didn't go backstage to change. She went directly to the bar.

Daniel was slumped on his stool, his head resting on one arm stretched across the bar, his hand still curved around a glass.

She gently removed the glass from his hand, then spoke to the bartender.

"Can you help me with him, Kevin?"

"Sure thing, Skylar. Who is he?"

She wasn't about to mention his name. The Westmorelands were a prominent family, the kind the gossips would love to see brought down a notch or two. Besides that, she figured nearly everybody in Vicksburg would know that Daniel was a minister, and she wasn't about to be the one to put a black mark on his record.

"Just a guy I know."

"What do you want me to do with him?"

"Help me get him to my car."

Kevin had the weight and build of a good-sized refrigerator, which was a very good thing, for even though Skylar was tall she wouldn't have been a match for Daniel. She wondered if he'd ever played football. He certainly had the body for it.

Most of which was now draped over her in the most provocative way. In a way that made her face warm and the rest of her downright hot.

Lord, what was she getting herself into? What was she going to do with Daniel once she got him home?

When they went through the door and the rain hit his face, he roused long enough to lift his head and mutter, "Wha's happenin'?"

"Nothing," Skylar said. "Go back to sleep."

"Which seat?" Kevin asked. "Front or back?"

"Better put him up front with me." There was no telling what he'd do if he roused back there all by himself.

She stood back while Kevin dumped Daniel into the front seat. He didn't ask how she was going to get him out when she got home, and it was a very good thing, for Skylar didn't know either.

"Will you need me for anything else, Skylar?"

"No, thank you, Kevin."

"I can follow you home if you like, help you get him inside."

"Thanks, but no. Go on home to Margie. I'll bet she's waiting up for you."

Kevin got a big grin on his face that made Skylar feel lonesome for things she'd never even known she was missing.

"She always does." He escorted her around the car, then stood in the rain watching until she was out of the parking lot.

As she turned the curve, Daniel tilted sideways then lay there with his head resting on her shoulder. Suddenly, for no reason at all, Skylar began to cry. Call it rainy-day blues, call it late-night doldrums, call it any darned thing you wanted.

She drove and let the tears come.

Chapter Eleven

Parked in her driveway with the motor running and the windshield wipers swishing, Skylar leaned over and touched Daniel's face.

"Daniel, wake up. We're home."

"Wha…"

He peered at her through squinted eyes, then gave a huge and beautiful smile and pulled her into his arms.

"Daniel…"

She tried to push herself out of his arms but couldn't, so she just decided to make the best of it.

"We have to go inside now," she said.

"It can wait."

She told herself she didn't see his kiss coming. She told herself she didn't have time to duck.

Lies, her conscience said, and she told it to shut up.

The simple truth was she'd seen what was coming, she'd

had time to dodge…and she hadn't. She wanted him to kiss her. Wanted it with every fiber of her being.

Such a kiss. She'd never known anything like it, never felt such sensations. Skyrockets went off in her head. A parade complete with a brass band and elephants carrying bespangled trapeze artists marched across her heart. A pair of snow-white doves grabbed her spirit and soared toward the night-dark sky.

They kissed until the windows were steamed, and so was she. Daniel, too, from the looks of it.

Her skirt had crawled up her legs and he put a hand on her bare thigh. A hot hand. A hand that knew just how to touch a woman.

Daniel, stop that, is what she should say. Instead she wrapped her arms around him for another kiss. Just one more, and then she'd go inside.

She'd be a good girl. For once in her life.

And all because of Daniel.

Not only did she *not* want a preacher—certainly not for the long haul—but she didn't want to be responsible for the downfall of one. Skylar didn't draw the line at many things, but at this one, she did.

She'd take the rap for all sorts of misdeeds that affected only herself. But she wasn't about to add leading preachers astray to her long list of sins.

And so she contented herself with melting against him, reveling in the feel of being held close against a chest that had to rank right up there with the broadest and the best. Besides, he had chest hair. Which she adored. Enticing bits of sun-kissed chest hair peeping over the top of his white shirt which had managed to come partially unbuttoned.

God, she adored an olive-skinned man in a white shirt. Daniel was not only gorgeous in his: he was lethal. There ought to be a law against men such as he wearing white shirts around women such as she. Women who couldn't resist.

She didn't even try. She buried her fingers in those crisp dark hairs and let herself dream a million dreams.

What the heck. It was raining, it was dark and there was no one around to see. Not that she cared. She'd have done the same thing even if she'd been standing in the middle of a crowded airport. With fifteen hundred morally upright citizens watching.

Daniel mumbled something incoherent, then leaned over her and slid his open mouth from her throat down to her cleavage. And beyond.

Her straps fell off her shoulders, the top of her gown slid down and his mouth closed over one tight nipple. Skylar groaned. How could she help herself? As Daniel wove his magic spell, she buried her hands in his hair and pulled him close. Close enough so that she melted against his skin, melted against his hot tongue.

What was happening to her? Here she was necking in the front seat of her Thunderbird as if she were a teenager. And loving every minute of it. Not wanting to stop. Not *ever* wanting to stop.

His mouth still plying its magic, he pushed her gown lower and kneaded her other breast. Skylar was a wild thing, wet and shaken, exploding, losing control.

Losing control.

"Daniel." She pushed her hands against his shoulders. "We have to stop now."

"Can't stop....don't want to."

He slipped his hand under her gown, searching, seeking, sliding inside.

"Daniel...don't."

"Don't you want it?"

"Yes..." She wanted it more than anything she could ever remember wanting. "No. No, I don't."

She shoved forcefully enough to break contact.

He looked at her like a little boy who'd had his Christmas puppy ripped out of his arms. She would have laughed if she hadn't been so hot and bothered. And so upset with herself.

What had she been thinking of? Playing with fire that way?

It didn't take a Philadelphia lawyer to figure that out. She'd always played with fire. Half the time that's what kept her going, the sheer adrenaline high she gained from always doing the unconventional thing, from walking on the wild side, from seeing just how far out on a limb she could get without falling off and breaking herself.

"We have to go inside now, Daniel."

"Can't. Don' wanna go home."

"This is not your house. It's mine."

She pulled her gown back onto her shoulders and smoothed down her skirt. Lord, she was burning up. Roasting in this hot car. She had to have air. She had to have relief.

When she got inside she was going to turn the air conditioner on. Full blast. She was going to turn the thermostat so low she'd think she was in the Alaskan tundra.

"We're going inside now, Daniel. Can you walk?"

"Don' wanna walk. Wanna make love."

He reached for her and she slapped at his hands.

"Behave now, Daniel." She reached behind her, found the door handle, eased open the door. "I'm getting out of the car now."

"Don' leave...."

"I'm not leaving you. I'm coming around to the other side of the car, and we're going into my house."

"Not mine?"

"No, not yours. Mine. We're going in there together."

He flashed that beautiful smile, the one that made him look like a little boy about to ride his first pony.

"Okay."

"Fine, then."

He launched across the seat and latched on, hands, lips and all.

Oh, help.

His kisses melted her. Stole her breath. Stole her will. It was that simple. That wonderful.

And that terrible.

This simply wouldn't do. She had to get him inside. She had to get him in bed.

But not hers. Definitely not hers. For she knew as surely as she knew her name that if she ever let this man into her bed, if she ever made love with him, she was lost.

Forever.

There would be no more Skylar, woman living alone with her cat, woman free as a breeze to hit the open road any time she liked, without encumbrances. There would be Skylar, one of a pair, Skylar attached heart and soul with a man called Daniel, the most highly inappropriate man she could think of.

Somewhere in heaven—if there was such a place—her daddy must be laughing his head off. She wouldn't put it past him to have been the brains behind all this. Somehow he'd managed to talk Saint Peter into sending Daniel Westmoreland her way.

Her daddy couldn't win her soul with all his preaching so he was trying to sneak in the back door and win her with romancing.

Well, no thank you very much. She wasn't fixing to stand by and be an easy target. She was simply going to get this big gorgeous man into her house, let him sleep off his alcoholic stupor and then send him on his way.

Back to his pulpit. None the worse for wear. His honor still intact.

She wedged her hands between them and shoved with all her might. When they split apart, he gave her an aggrieved look.

"Wha'd I do?"

"Just sit still, Daniel. Don't move!"

Skylar bailed out, hurried around the car and jerked the door open.

"You can come out now."

"Don' wanna."

What in the world was she going to do? She couldn't leave him out there all night. Somebody might come along and see him. Some nosey gossip.

Or worse. Somebody might steal her car. With him in it. Somebody with a knife or a gun.

Lord, if she ever got inside she was going to have to take something to calm her nerves. What? *What?* She wasn't a pill-popping woman. She wasn't the kind of woman who had an ailment for every occasion and knew fifteen remedies for them all.

A cup of tea. That was it. She'd drink a cup of hot tea. Or was it hot milk?

Where were wise and kindly grandmothers when you needed them?

"Daniel, if I have to lean into that car and drag you out it won't be a pretty sight."

He found that uproariously funny. Skylar stamped her foot at him.

"Daniel Westmoreland, you stop that laughing and get out of the car. For God's sake, it's raining."

"Don' take the Lord'sh name in vain." He shook his

finger at her, then hiccupped and covered his mouth. "'Scuse me."

"I'm getting wet out here, Daniel. And I'm mad as hell. And if you say one word about watching my language, I'm going to leave you out here all by yourself."

"You're a hard-hearted woman," he said, but he heaved himself upright and stumbled out of the car.

Skylar caught him before he toppled, though how she did that she didn't know. A big man like Daniel. And a slender woman like her.

They say that when you're put in stressful situations you're capable of great deeds. For instance, lifting the front end of a car.

That's what it felt like struggling up the rain-slick driveway with Daniel leaning heavily on her. Supporting several thousand pounds of tempered steel.

By the time she got him through the front door, she was panting. She leaned back to rest, and he came with her. Face to face, chest to chest, groin to groin.

Speaking of tempered steel...

"Lord, help me," she muttered.

"Skylar..." Daniel was fumbling with the top of her dress again. "Sky..."

"Stop that."

"Donchou like it?"

"It's not a matter of what I like or dislike." Now, why had she said that? Why hadn't she just said no?

She pushed herself away from the door and tugged him toward the spare bedroom.

"So far, so good. Just keep moving those legs, Daniel. A few more steps, and we'll be there."

He fell heavily onto the bed, taking her with him. She was so tired she thought about just lying there, resting her head on his chest and closing her eyes and simply falling asleep.

Of course, there were a few glitches in that plan, not the least of which was his obvious arousal. She'd never be able to shut her eyes, scrunched up next to that.

"Now," she said, trying to sound all business and failing. "I'm going to take off your shoes and tuck some covers around you, and you're going to get a nice night's sleep."

"Don' wanna shleep."

She untangled herself from him, which wasn't as easy as it sounded, considering that he didn't want to be untangled and kept trying to hold her captive, octopus-like, all questing arms and legs.

Finally she was upright, both feet planted firmly on the floor and he was on the bed. The picture of innocence.

Skylar resisted the urge to smooth back his hair. She didn't dare get that close to his hands again. Instead she walked to the foot of the bed and removed his shoes, taking note that he had big feet.

What was it they always said about men with big feet?

Oh, mercy, she didn't want to know. Didn't want even to think about that.

She grabbed a quilt from the top of the closet and threw it over him.

"Good night, Daniel," she said, then practically ran from the room.

He was saying something, but she didn't wait to hear. She didn't stop until she was safe in her bedroom.

Or was she? Memories were no respecters of walls.

She stripped her wet dress off, hung it over the shower rail to dry, though what good that was going do, she didn't know. It was probably ruined. All those sequins.

Skylar climbed into bed and pulled the covers up to her

chin. She had bigger things to worry about than ruining a five-hundred-dollar dress. Bigger, as in six feet tall. Possibly more. A hundred eighty pounds. Give or take a few. A killer smile, and kisses to die for.

Groaning, Skylar tossed and turned, tangling the covers around herself so that she felt like a mummy.

A loud thump in the next room jerked her upright.

"Daniel!"

Had she slept? She must have for the luminous hands on the clock were pointing to three o'clock.

She sat there with the covers pulled up to her chin, listening. There was another loud thump, followed by a muttered oath.

Skylar rushed into the spare room and found Daniel upright, though just barely. Wearing not a stitch. His clothes were strewn about the room, mostly on the floor, as if a strong wind had flung them there.

Or a strong pair of arms. A muscular, sun-bronzed pair of arms that had held her in a way that melted her heart.

"Daniel, what are you doing out of the bed?"

"Skylar? Where am I?"

"You're in my house. You were too drunk to go home so I brought you here."

The room was dim, with only the feeble light leaking through from the bathroom to illuminate the two people who faced each other. Suddenly aware. Suddenly tense with the knowledge that Daniel was naked and Skylar almost.

They reached out at the same time, Daniel for his shorts and Skylar for his white shirt. Her hair hid her flaming face as she struggled with the tiny buttons.

Leave. Why couldn't she just walk out and leave him standing there?

Because he might need me.

He was still a little stumbly, his speech a little slurred.

Who was she trying to kid? She couldn't leave because she might need him. Need him with an urgency that stole her reason.

His eyes were deep dark pools, sucking her in. If she didn't leave soon she would drown.

"If you don't need me, I guess I'll be going."

She raced toward the door, almost made it through when he stopped her.

"Don't go."

She turned back to him, knowing she shouldn't, knowing she couldn't help herself.

"Please...Sky..."

He held out his hand and she moved toward him slowly, a moth headed toward flames.

Chapter Twelve

From the diary of Anne Beaufort Westmoreland:

September 23, 2001

Sometime in the middle of the night I felt the change in Michael. I was in bed with him...(yes, that's what I said, in the bed with Michael. I don't care who doesn't like it. He's my husband. More than that, he's my love, and that's where we belong. Together.)

Anyway, I was lying there with my hand over his heart so I could make sure it kept beating, when all of a sudden I felt this awareness in him. That's the only way I can describe it. Awareness, as if suddenly Michael had returned to his body, as if suddenly he had decided to fight the pneumonia, to fight his way back to me.

He's coming back to us. I just know it.

That's what I told Emily when she and Jake came in early this morning.

"Do you think so, Mom?" she asked.

"I know so, Em. And don't you ever forget it."

I'm glad Jake's with her. He's levelheaded and steady. Just what Emily needs. More than that, he loves her extravagantly.

This morning she talked of postponing the wedding, waiting until Michael comes out of his coma, but I told her, "You aren't going to do any such thing. I'm not going to let you and Jake put your life on hold. Besides, your father needs a deadline, something to inspire him to wake up and get out of that bed."

Jake has taken her downtown now so they can make a few arrangements. They didn't say what. I assume they'll be talking to florists and whatnot. Of course, Daniel will perform the ceremony.

And speaking of Daniel, here's what Emily said to me this morning:

"Daniel didn't come home last night."

"What do you mean, didn't come home?"

"Exactly that. He wasn't there when Jake and I got in from the airport. We waited for him to come down to breakfast, and when he didn't show up I got worried and went upstairs to check. His bed hasn't even been slept in."

"Don't worry. Daniel's a grown man. He can take care of himself."

That's what I told Emily, "Don't worry." Naturally, I can't help but worry, myself. So much has happened lately that I keep expecting disaster around every corner.

Clarice knows what a fussbudget I've become. "You've got to stop that," she told me yesterday. "Now you listen to me, Anne Westmoreland, you're the most optimistic person I know and I'm not going to let you turn into some old prune-faced pessimist right before my very eyes."

That got a rise out of me. "Prune-faced!" I yelled, and she burst into this glorious, full-bodied laugh that had everybody in the nursing home turning their heads and smiling, which just goes to show that there's not enough laughter in nursing homes.

Something ought to be done about that. They say laughter is the best medicine.

Come to think of it, I'm the one who can do something about that. Michael loves those old Laurel and Hardy movies. We used to cuddle together on the bed and laugh our heads off at the antics of those two. What great comedians.

When Emily and Jake get back I'll send them home to get a few of those old movies, then I'll turn on the VCR and sit beside Michael's bed and laugh my head off. Hoping he'll hear. Hoping he'll want to laugh, too.

Or maybe I'll call home and see if Daniel can bring one. If he's home...

Chapter Thirteen

Two things awakened Daniel: the sun pouring through the window and the awareness of a warm body curled next to him.

He eased his eyes open, then quickly shut them against the pain that hammered his head. He was going to have a doozy of a hangover, something he hadn't dealt with since the wild days of his youth.

Of more immediate concern were the woman sleeping in his arms—in his shirt, as a matter of fact—and his libido. Fully functioning. Calling attention to itself. Demanding relief.

Lord have mercy. What was he going to do?

More to the point, what had he done?

Last night was a blur. He clearly remembered going into a place called Babe's. He remembered his first drink, and how he'd almost choked on alcohol and guilt. The second had gone down easier. And the third. After that…God only knew…

Did He?

Daniel eased his eyes shut. Even blinking too fast made his head pound.

He was in no condition to do any soul-searching. The only condition he was in was an embarrassing one. Doubly so, because Skylar was waking up. Slowly. Causing Daniel further consternation.

She arched her back like a cat, and every delectable inch of her body rubbed against him—her silky arms, her long, long legs, her soft breasts, her…

Lord have mercy, he didn't want to even think about that. There was only so much temptation a man could stand.

Had he? Had he withstood temptation last night? If so, what was she doing in his bed?

Actually, it was her bed. Had to be. There were no brass beds at Belle Rose. Furthermore, he'd left the nursing home with the full intention of avoiding going back there, going back and playing the game: Daniel Westmoreland, steady, reliable, dependable, a port in every storm, leader of his flock, interim leader of his family, a man who had all the answers.

Hell, he didn't have one single answer. Furthermore, that was the first time he'd even thought a byword in…how many years was it? Seven? Eight?

Skylar stretched once more, raising her arms and throwing her head back in a big yawn. She looked adorable. Good enough to eat. And that's what he wanted to do. Nibble on every inch of her, starting with her shapely toes.

Any minute now she would be fully awake. She'd open her eyes and see him. What should he do? Leap out of bed and grab his clothes? No, that would be cowardly. Furthermore, they were so entangled any small movement would jar her awake, and he didn't want to do that.

There was only one thing to do: lie there and face the music.

Skylar felt so safe and cozy she didn't even want to open her eyes. And so she didn't.

She hadn't awakened with that feeling in a long time. Not since early childhood. Way back to the days of innocence.

Anyhow, she'd never been one to face the day with a bang. She liked to ease into her day. Stick a toe outside and test the waters. Run around naked awhile so she could get used to being in her own skin once more.

And so she cuddled back down into her good warm spot and let herself drift, dreaming.... There was a strong pair of arms wrapped 'round her (Yum!) and a broad chest pillowing her cheek, lots of good-smelling chest hair...oh, she loved this. She was never going to open her eyes.

Never.

Until this very minute she hadn't realized how tired she was of waking up in a bed all by herself. Of being alone. Adrift in a murky cosmic fog, one against the world.

She lay securely in a pleasant half-dreaming state until something inside her triggered an alarm. She snapped open her eyes, then lay there with reality crashing down around her.

This was no dream; this was real. She was lying in bed cuddled up to a *preacher*. Lord help her, what had she been thinking last night? Apparently she hadn't been thinking at all.

"Good morning."

Daniel sounded as casual as if the two of them had accidentally met over coffee at the doughnut shop instead of waking up tangled together in the bed.

"Good morning," she said, and then they stared at each other until both their faces flushed with the knowledge of where they were and how close they were.

Lord! if they got any closer she'd faint. It was that simple, that terrifying, that wonderful.

Here was a man who looked glorious in the morning sun. Disheveled hair, beard stubble, sensational bare chest and all.

Skylar fought the urge to run her hands over his chest, to tangle her fingers in his chest hair and give a little tug, then bend over, kiss it and make it better.

Daniel saved her by starting to separate their various body parts. Skylar scooted to the far side of the bed, then noticed the direction of Daniel's gaze. His shirt was unbuttoned about halfway down and gaping enough to put most of her torso on full display.

She pulled the sheet up to her chin, and he pulled it above his waist. But not before she got an eyeful.

"I'm afraid I don't remember much about last night," he said.

"No, you wouldn't."

"I apologize for that."

"Don't. I like a man with enough faults to be human."

"How did I get here?"

"You said you didn't want to go home, so I rescued you."

He chuckled. "You rescued me?"

"I don't see anything so funny about that."

"It's not funny, it's delightful. You have one of the kindest hearts I've ever known."

"Well, don't tell anybody. I don't want to ruin my reputation."

''Your secret is safe with me.''

She gave him a wicked smile. ''And yours is safe with me.''

His smile vanished, and deep color flushed his face.

''I don't quite know how to say this,'' he said.

''Go ahead. I've heard it all. Nothing shocks me.''

''Did anything happen here last night?''

Skylar thought of several ways she could reply. No, she could say, but if we don't get out of this bed soon something's going to.

That would send him scurrying. And in a hurry.

Or she could say, Hmmmm, Yummy! then watch him twist in the winds of guilt.

If she wanted to. Which she didn't. She had no desire to make Daniel Westmoreland feel any worse than he already did.

Skylar sighed. If she didn't watch herself she was going to turn into a boring, conventional woman.

''If you mean, did you do anything that would force me to make an honest man of you, the answer is no.''

If he looked relieved she was going to kill him. Fortunately, all he did was have the grace to look chagrined. Skylar couldn't resist one last word.

''Believe me, Daniel, if anything had happened in this bed last night, you'd remember.''

With that last word she flounced out of bed and marched out of the bedroom.

Let him chew on that for a while. She had things to do, places to go, people to see. Besides that, she had to get dressed.

And, she hoped, so would he. Just the thought of him sitting in there half-naked was enough to put her in a snit. On the way to her bedroom she scowled at the cat and kicked a footstool, just for good measure.

Then she realized she was still wearing Daniel's shirt, which meant he didn't have anything to cover his fabulous chest, and that made her even madder.

"Well, hell." She jerked the shirt off and grabbed her robe then marched back in there to deliver his clothes.

Too late, she realized she hadn't knocked. Daniel was standing in the middle of the room, one foot in his pants and one out. Chest bare. Great legs. Delicious looking.

"I brought your shirt."

"Thanks."

Their eyes locked, and all of a sudden it got too hot in the room. Skylar hung his shirt on the doorknob and fled.

So far, so good. Now she just had to get through the next few minutes till she could get him out of the house. She dressed quickly in the oldest, scruffiest sweatshirt she could find and a comfortable pair of faded jeans, not too tight. She didn't want to appear the least bit provocative.

Not that anything would happen between her and Daniel while he was stone-cold sober. She was the last woman in the world he'd want to get involved with. Completely wrong for him in every way.

Not the least of which was her profession.

She went into the kitchen with Pussy Willow stalking along behind her, decidedly miffed. Cats don't take well to being ignored. Especially this cat. Pussy Willow considered herself queen of the house, and woe unto Skylar if she forgot.

She poured gourmet cat food into a china dish then said, "Here, kitty, kitty."

Pussy Willow turned her back, ignoring Skylar. She hated being called kitty. Her whole attitude said, *I have a name, thank you very much, and I'd appreciate it if you'd use it.*

"Okay, Pussy Willow. I give up. I'm going to leave your

food here and you can eat it or not. I don't care. I have more important things on my mind.''

''Pussy Willow?''

Skylar jumped as if she'd been shot. Daniel was standing in the doorway fully dressed and still every bit as appealing as he had been without clothes.

Oh, help.

''Yes. I named her that because I found her underneath a willow tree.'' She made a face. ''Not very creative, I know.''

''She's a beautiful cat.''

''Don't tell her that. She already has a big head.''

Daniel laughed, then put his hands on his temples.

''I wonder if I could trouble you for an aspirin? I seem to have a headache.''

''I don't wonder. There's some in the top left drawer of the vanity in the guest bathroom.''

''Thanks.''

He left, walking as if every step hurt. Skylar knew just how he felt.

The night she'd come back from Europe and found they'd buried her father she'd consoled herself with half a bottle of wine. And she didn't even drink. Not much, anyhow. And never more than one glass. Two was enough to put her three sheets to the wind.

When Daniel returned, she handed him a concoction she'd mixed—tomato juice, red-hot sauce, bits of onion, a squirt of lemon.

''What is it?''

''Hair of the dog.''

''Does that mean don't ask?''

''Yes. Just drink it fast and drink it all.''

He passed it under his nose, sniffing, then made a face. She laughed.

"You can hold your nose if you like," she said.

Daniel upended his glass and then raced to the bathroom gagging.

"You look a little pale around the gills," she said when he came back.

"If you weren't my angel rescuer I'd say you did that deliberately."

She loved it when he called her his angel. Now why was that? She'd never been one for pet names. Skylar was alarmed. Spend one night with Daniel, and she was turning into a sentimental woman.

Lord, what would she do next?

She knew what she had to do—get him out of her house, and then out of her life. Any way she could. He was far, far too dangerous.

"I suppose my car is still at the club?" Daniel said.

"Yes. It's safe, though. Pete runs a tight ship."

"Pete?"

"Pete Sanford, the owner. He's an old friend of mine. From the early days of the band."

"I know him. Played football with him in high school."

So Daniel *had* played football. Not that it mattered. Skylar didn't want to know any more about him than she already did.

"I'll take you down there to pick it up."

"You don't have to do that. I can get a cab."

"I don't mind. I need to get out anyhow. I don't have anything to eat in this house except cat food or I'd offer you some breakfast."

"Just the thought of food makes me queasy."

Suddenly he was across the kitchen, holding her hand. Skylar felt the shock all the way to her toes.

"I can never thank you enough for everything you did for me last night, Skylar."

"I would say, anytime, but you're not the kind of man who needs rescuing except under extreme circumstances." The look he gave her turned her to putty. "I'll get my car keys."

They didn't say much in the car, though Daniel still had a dozen questions tumbling through his mind. He wanted to ask more about last night, about how they'd ended up in bed together, but he figured it was best to let sleeping dogs lie, particularly that one.

When they got to the parking lot, she turned to him and put her hand on his arm.

"Daniel, I want you to know that I won't say a word about last night. To anyone."

"You're more than generous."

"Don't pin any medals on me."

There was nothing left to say except goodbye. Daniel thanked her once again, and as he was leaving her car, she called out his name.

"Daniel…" He leaned into the car so he could see her face. "You're a good man, and nothing that happened last night should make you doubt your ability to continue your ministry."

"Thank you, Skylar."

She gave him the victory sign. "Onward and upward, preacherman."

Daniel stood in the parking lot watching until she had disappeared, and then he climbed in his car and drove to Belle Rose, hoping no one was home.

He needed a shower and a shave, but most of all he needed some time to himself before he had to go back to the nursing home and faced his family. Not that they would question him. About anything. He was fortunate to have the most accepting, most loving family on the face of the earth.

But at the moment, their needs exceeded his capacity. He had nothing left to offer them. He was used up. Empty. A boat stripped of its moorings, adrift on an unknown sea.

Chapter Fourteen

Daniel saw the message light when he walked through the door. It was a call from Hannah.

"I'll be coming into the airport at two. Don't bother to pick me up. I'll rent a car. I'll need one anyhow."

That was good news and bad. Hannah was a strong woman, and she'd be wonderful support for their mother. Just being in the same room with Hannah was like standing in front of a bracing ocean breeze. On the other hand, she'd see right through Daniel. His mother and Emily were soft, gentle women, easygoing, never prying.

Hannah was astute and observant, and considered it her duty to make sure every member of her family was on the right path. In her view, problems were not merely to be solved; they were to be tackled, wrestled to the ground, subdued and crushed out.

One look at Daniel and she'd be off on a crusade to set him straight. And he didn't even like to think of her meeting Skylar. Lord have mercy. Two strong-willed woman. It would be a clash of Titans.

Unless Hannah was too distracted by Michael's condition to notice....

"Fat chance," Daniel muttered.

Then, supporting his head with the palms of his hands, Daniel went upstairs to make himself presentable enough to face his family.

When he got to the nursing home, Daniel found Hannah and his mother sitting beside Michael's bed watching an old movie and laughing their heads off.

"Come on over here, Daniel. We're watching Laurel and Hardy. Michael loves them." His mother smoothed back his father's hair. "Don't you, darling?"

Hannah shot him a look that said, Mother's losing touch here, and Daniel was quick to defend her.

"That's a great idea, Mom. You never know what will trigger an awakening." He gave Hannah a quick hug. "Hey, big sis."

"Hey, yourself, and don't call me sis. You look like hell."

"Thanks." Hannah was deliberately baiting him with that kind of language, but Daniel refused to bite. Instead he pulled a chair to the other side of the bed, sat down with considerable relief and said, "Hey, Dad, how's it going?"

He'd forgotten how much a night of carousing took out of a man.

"Here comes the good part," Anne said, then much to Daniel's relief she took up a running commentary, leaning close to the bed, speaking in tender tones, stroking Michael and laughing softly.

Watching them, Daniel's heart ached. Not just for his

parents, but for himself, as well. Would he ever know such love?

Skylar came unbidden to his mind. The way she'd looked in her blue sequined gown standing in the smoky bar singing. And in the car....

With his mother's gentle murmuring as background, memories blossomed as surely as long-buried seeds seeking the sun. Of how he'd kissed Skylar. And where. And how it had felt. Like being reborn. Like paradise.

He remembered waking in the middle of the night, constricted by his clothing, disoriented, then falling against the brass footrail. And she was there, standing barefoot and reaching for his white shirt.

Suddenly, he'd known he couldn't be alone. He'd held out his hand to her and she'd come to him, come to him with a soft smile on her lips. Then he'd wrapped his arms around her and led her to the bed....

And slept the sweetest sleep of his life.

It felt like love. Like the kind of love that would last a lifetime and beyond. A sweet loving, giving relationship that would stand strong against any slings and arrows the world might toss their way.

And slings and arrows would come. Of that Daniel had no doubt. He could even name a likely source or two. Not the least of which was his pastor/parish relations committee.

"Daniel...?"

The movie was over, it was quiet in the room and Hannah was staring at him as if he'd lost his mind. In a way, he had. Here he was daydreaming about a relationship with Skylar Tate when she hated his profession and merely tolerated him.

Or did she? If memory served, she'd kissed him with as much passion as he'd felt when he'd kissed her.

"I'm sorry, Hannah. What were you saying?"

"Where were you, bro?"

When? Last night?

"Woolgathering," he said, hoping to get by with it.

Hannah gave him another look, then let his remark slide.

"I asked if you wanted to take your big sister out to dinner tonight?"

"Sure. What about Em and Jake?"

"Those two are so wrapped up in each other they don't even know we're on the same planet. Besides, they said they wanted to come here and spend some time with Mom and Dad this evening."

"They're bringing catfish and hushpuppies." Anne laughed. "I'm going to get fat with all this attention." As always she turned to include Michael in the conversation. "If you don't wake up soon, darling, you won't even know me. I'm turning into a roly-poly."

"Don't believe a word she says, Dad," Hannah chimed in. "She's gorgeous. If I looked like Mom I'd have men crawling all over me."

The lively give-and-take seemed so normal that for a moment Daniel *believed* again, believed in the power of miracles, the power of hope, the power of love.

"Don't believe it, Dad. If Hannah had men clamoring for her attention, she'd be knocking them off with a ten-foot shillelagh."

"I don't know so much about that, Daniel," his mother said. "Hannah's a strong, independent woman, but she has a lot of love to give."

"I'd like to meet the man who can win our Hannah."

"Help, Dad," Hannah said. "I'm outnumbered."

Jake and Emily arrived in the midst of the friendly bantering, holding hands, smiling and bearing food.

"What's so funny in here?" Emily asked.

Hannah and Daniel pointed to each other, then cracked up again. Anne finally shooed them out the door.

"Where do you want to eat?" Daniel asked when they were outside in the parking lot.

"The Biscuit Company Café. I've been dreaming about one of their po'boys ever since I left Yellowstone."

"We'll take my car," Daniel said, expecting an argument. Hannah always liked to be in charge.

"Fine." She slid into the passenger side. "Maybe they'll have a good blues band playing," she said, and Daniel immediately thought of Skylar.

"Hey, where'd you go?"

"Woolgathering again."

"I don't buy it." Hannah twisted around so she could study him. "What's going on with you, Daniel?"

"Why do you ask?"

"God, I *hate* it when you do that. Answer a question with a question. You know very well what I mean, and don't think you can weasel out of an answer, because you can't."

All of a sudden Daniel realized that he needed somebody to talk to. Not just anybody, but Hannah. She might offer him unsolicited advice; she might tell him things he didn't want to hear, but in the end she would accept whatever decision he made because she believed in him and she loved him unconditionally.

There was a certain comfort in that, in knowing that he was part of a family with strong bonds. Why had he ever believed he was adrift? As long as he had a family who loved him, he was always tethered to a safe port.

"I'll tell you as soon as we get to the restaurant."

And he would. At least part of it.

As soon as their orders were taken he leaned toward his older sister.

"I've met a woman," he said.

"Who is she?"

"Skylar Tate."

"Skylar Tate? The singer?" He nodded. "The star of that hot video…what's it called?"

Every muscle he had was knotted; every nerve ending twanging.

"Yes. That Skylar Tate."

Hannah laughed so hard she had to wipe her face with her napkin, while Daniel sat like a man turned to stone. This could be either a very good sign or his worst nightmare come true. He didn't attempt to interrupt her interlude of hilarity, but waited for it to end.

"Thank God," she said. "I was afraid you were going to get stuck with some little Miss Goody Two-shoes who was so sanctimonious she wouldn't even blow her nose on Sunday."

"Then you approve?" Daniel didn't know why that should surprise him. The Westmorelands could never be accused of conventionality.

"Wholeheartedly. When can I meet her?"

"I don't know."

"You don't know?"

"I said I like this woman; I didn't say she liked me back."

"What's not to like?"

"She hates preachers."

"Why?"

"Her father was one, apparently one of those hidebound moralists who disapproved of everything his daughter did."

"That had to be tough on her."

Hannah looked out the window at the river for a while, mulling over the problem the way she always did, and when she turned back and smiled, Daniel realized just how beautiful she was. Spectacular, really. He would have been amazed that at thirty-two his sister was still unattached if he hadn't known that her love for adventure superseded everything else. Except family.

And in that respect, she was a carbon copy of their father.

"What's she like, Daniel?" Hannah finally asked.

"Unconventional, as you would expect. Feisty. Strong-willed."

"I like this girl already."

"And she has one of the softest, kindest hearts I've ever known."

"Women like that are easily hurt, Daniel."

"I know. I would never do anything to hurt her."

"I know you wouldn't. Furthermore, I know you would never try to change her into some prissy little wimp who would meet with everybody's approval."

"By *everybody,* you mean my congregation?"

"Precisely."

"No. I would never do that."

What he didn't tell Hannah, what he couldn't tell anyone was that he wasn't sure he'd have a congregation once he returned to Atlanta. Not because of what had happened at Babe's, but because of what was happening inside his own heart and soul.

"If you really want Skylar Tate, don't let anything stand in your way. Not *anything.* Do you understand me?"

"Yes."

She wasn't talking merely about differences between him and Skylar, but about their family's situation. She was saying to him the same thing he'd heard Anne say to Emily. *Life goes on.*

Hannah reached across the table and squeezed his hand.

"Daniel, don't let this one get away."

Chapter Fifteen

From the diary of Anne Beaufort Westmoreland:

September 23, 2001

It's quiet now. All the children have gone, Emily and Jake back to Belle Rose, and probably Hannah and Daniel, too, by now. As much as I love having them all here, I enjoy my time alone with Michael.

The doctor came back around ten and said he was showing a slight improvement, which is encouraging. Of course, I didn't need a doctor to tell me that. I felt it myself, early this morning.

Clarice called a little while ago. She's still worried about me. I told her she was worrying about the wrong person, that Michael was the one she should be thinking about. She says I'm losing my spark, and that tomorrow while the children are here to stay with Michael (she knows good and well I'm not going to leave him alone) she's going to take me to get a manicure and a facial even if she has to drag me kicking and screaming.

I admit I could use both, but what I really want to do is clean house. Top to bottom. Oh, I know. I know. I have a housekeeper. More than a housekeeper, really. Sissy June's been with the Beaufort family so long she's more like family to me than some of mother's sisters.

Anyhow...back to cleaning my house. I feel the need to get Michael's study shipshape. (He has always been so well-organized. Almost a neatnik. But then, I guess that's what comes of years of climbing mountains. He learned to pare down to the essentials. And God knows, he had to be organized. There's no such thing as taking time to search for an ice ax in the midst of a climb.)

But more than cleaning, I feel the need to touch his books, to read his journals, his diaries (he's better than I at recording events). If I can find them.

And I want Clarice to be with me when I do. Not the children. I don't want them to see me cry. And I know I'll cry if (no, when) I find my precious husband's personal papers.

I know he won't mind. I know he'll understand.

Still, I'll tell him what I'm going to do. Tonight when I climb into bed beside him, I'll put my arms around his still-strong chest and say, "Darling, I'm losing touch with you. I don't know what you're thinking anymore, and I'm scared. I need something to bring back a sense that you are present, and that's why I'm going to go prying into your private papers.

"Tell me it's all right, my love. Give me some sign. Anything. *Please*."

I'm feeling desperate again, and I think Clarice senses

that. I told her about watching the old Laurel and Hardy comedies, and how we all laughed. I confessed to her that my laughter was as fake as crocodile tears. That I was doing it for the children as much as for Michael.

She said to me, "Anne what you need is a good cry. And I know I do. I know."

But I can't cry. Not yet. There is another night to get through. Another night holding onto the shell of my beloved.

I'll cry tomorrow.

Chapter Sixteen

Daniel and Hannah didn't leave the Biscuit Company Café until after ten, and when he turned onto the driveway at Belle Rose, his sister grabbed his arm.

"Stop the car," she said.

"What's wrong?"

"Nothing. I just want to drink it all in." She sighed. "I always forget how beautiful Belle Rose is. God, look at that moon, Daniel. Everything looks washed clean in the moonlight, doesn't it?"

"Yes." *Except our hearts and souls.* "Ready?" he asked, shifting the car into gear.

"Ready."

Instead of parking in the garage, he pulled up in front of the house. Hannah twisted around to study him.

"Aren't you coming in?"

"No. I'm going to Babe's...to see Skylar."

"Good." Smiling, Hannah patted his arm. "I hope you

can get everything worked out, Daniel. And I mean *everything*."

So, he hadn't fooled his sister. Not that he'd expected to. She'd seen right through him, seen that something more was going on inside him than concern over a practically impossible relationship.

"Do you think Mom suspects anything?" he asked.

"No. She's totally wrapped up in Dad…Daniel, nobody expects miracles from you."

"You do have a knack for cutting to the heart of the matter, don't you?"

"I'm just like Dad. And so I'll take the liberty of speaking for him…get out of that rut and move forward, Daniel."

Daniel laughed. "You sound just like him."

"Yeah, well, I've been accused of having a whiskey voice. I tell them it's just my natural sexy self." She kissed him on the cheek. "Bye, bro. Have fun, and I mean *real* fun."

Daniel was relieved that he'd confided in her. What was it his dad had always said? *When you're faced with climbing a mountain, it's always best to have a dependable partner.*

He could count on Hannah, not only to be supportive, but to keep secrets, if necessary. And right now, the last thing he wanted the rest of his family to know was that the family's minister had taken to frequenting Babe's.

Skylar's rakish Thunderbird was in the parking lot. As he parked beside it, he wondered if he'd arrived in time for her last set.

Skylar was in the midst of one of her favorite torch songs when Daniel came in. "Come Rain or Come Shine." All of a sudden she knew what it meant, that old saying—*My heart stood still*—and the words of the song took on a meaning so personal her skin felt hot.

Gazing across the room she saw how it was possible to love a man as no one had ever loved, no matter what the circumstances. Were storms buffeting the house? Never mind, as long as you had each other. Was everybody who knew you opposed to the union? No problem, as long as the two of you stood together. Was the man in question a doctor of divinity and the woman a red-hot singer distinguishable from a stripper only by the tiniest wisp of clothing?

No amount of solidarity could hold back the storm of protest that would churn up.

Oh, help.

Skylar had done the unthinkable: she'd let her guard down and now she was in love with the one man in the world she could never have.

She knew what she had to do, but the idea of it made her almost physically ill. She had no heart for outrageous flirtation. She had no stomach for portraying herself as cheap and sleazy in front of Daniel Westmoreland.

But she had to. Didn't she?

Skylar got through her set, never taking her eyes off Daniel. Why not? As long as she was on stage she was safe. Untouchable.

The minute she left the stage, Pete cornered her.

"What's wrong, Sky? You look like you've seen a ghost."

"Worse."

"Want to tell an old pal about it?"

"It's Daniel Westmoreland. He's out there."

"Here? In Babe's? It can't be. I thought he was some hotshot preacher in a big church over in Atlanta."

"He is."

"I don't understand."

Skylar did. Only too well. She ruined everything she touched. It was that simple.

All of a sudden she started to cry. Pete gave her a clumsy hug, patted her back, and said, "Now, now, it can't be as bad as all that."

"It's worse." Sniffing, she leaned back and wiped her face on the handkerchief he handed her. "I've gone and fallen in love with him."

He pondered that for a while, his brow knit and his eyes squinted.

"What's so bad about that? Daniel Westmoreland is a great guy and you're the tops." He punched her playfully on the arm. "Hey, Sky. I think that's great."

Skylar didn't point out the obvious to him. After all, here was a man who believed in fairy tales. He described his wife as "the princess who kissed a frog" and his children as "his perfect angels." What could you expect from Pete except a rosy point of view on romance?

"Thanks, Pete." She gave him a smile.

"Hey, that's more like it. Can I get you anything before I go home?"

"No, thanks, Pete. I'm fine."

"You're sure?"

"You bet."

Skylar waited until Pete had left the club before she went onto the floor to launch her new act. Thank goodness, he wouldn't be around to see it. If she were lucky, she would have to do it only once.

That should be enough to send Daniel Westmoreland heading for the hills.

Daniel kept watching the side doors for Skylar. He knew she'd seen him. In fact, it seemed to him that she'd sung every love song straight to him. Wasn't it logical she'd come out to say hello? And if not that, wouldn't curiosity bring her out?

But no matter how hard he stared at the doors leading backstage, they remained firmly shut. He took a long swig of lemonade, trying to decide whether to keep waiting or to go charging backstage. Babe's was a small club. He wouldn't have any trouble finding her dressing room.

Then again, maybe she'd already gone home. Maybe she'd rushed to her car the minute she finished her set and was driving along in the moonlight with the top down.

He sat nursing his lemonade and trying to decide his next move, when all of a sudden the door on the right swung open and there was Skylar.

Lord have mercy, what was she wearing? Not much. That was for sure. The provocative red dress she'd worn on stage was staid by comparison. A tight little tube of a dress, so short it barely covered the subject. Bodice cut so low it didn't take any imagination at all to picture her breasts. Tiny straps he'd heard his sisters refer to as "spaghetti straps" holding the whole thing in place. And one of them slipped off her shoulder as she bent over the first table she came to.

Daniel thought she'd pop right out of her dress. Apparently so did the man she was talking to. He got this look on his face...like a man who'd won the sweepstakes. A *greedy* man.

Daniel banged his glass so hard onto the table the ice rattled.

Across the room Skylar ran her hand lightly through the man's hair then moved on, her strap sliding dangerously low, the front of her dress held up by gravity and two very seductive nipples. Clearly visible.

Daniel gripped his drink so hard it was a wonder he

didn't break the glass. Skylar's so-called dress was thin, almost sheer. And she was wearing nothing underneath except a minuscule thong.

By now every eye in the house was on her. She pranced across the crowded club, ignoring the men who called, "Hey, doll, over here, this way." She was headed straight to Daniel.

But not in a hurry to get there. That much was plain. Grabbing hands impeded her progress, but Skylar didn't seem to mind. In fact she encouraged it, stopping to lean way down low and chat, here patting a cheek, there bestowing a kiss on the top of a bald head. Pandemonium followed her. She left dozens of panting, openmouthed, boggle-eyed men in her wake.

When she came even with Daniel, she propped one hand on his table and purred, "Hello, preacherman. What're you doing here?"

She leaned dangerously low, and Daniel had no more control over the direction of his gaze than a robot operated by madmen.

"Watching the show."

"Good." Skylar looked into his eyes and for a moment she wavered.

Later Daniel would wonder if, in that brief moment, he could have done anything to change events. He would wonder...and regret.

Skylar slid into his lap, and the shock nearly jolted him from his chair. Instead, he sat perfectly still, holding onto his glass and his sanity by sheer force of will.

Out of the corner of his eye he noticed heads swiveled their way, hostile faces, envious eyes, greedy smirks. Hair on the back of his neck bristled, and the air tasted of trouble.

"What are you trying to do? Start a riot?"

"No, just a teeny, weeny little fire."

"Where?"

"Here." She executed a series of moves with her hips that had him gritting his teeth.

"You've succeeded."

"Good." She leaned close to his ear and whispered. "Why don't we see what we can do about it?"

"Here?"

"Backstage. In my dressing room. I have a little cot just for that purpose."

What was she trying to do?

Tempt him beyond any man's capacity to resist. That much was certain.

But Daniel saw more than the blatant seduction, more than the bold sensuality. Underneath her sleazy gold dress and her brazen ways, Daniel saw a vulnerable little girl who didn't believe in her own goodness, a scared little girl who would go to any lengths to keep from being hurt again.

He scooted her off his lap, stood up and grabbed her hand.

"Come on."

Her eyes widened and her face paled, but she recovered quickly and gave him a saucy smile.

"Eager beaver, aren't you? Oh, well, all of you are just alike."

Too disturbed to reply, he led her through the crowd, impeded at every turn by men grabbing her any place they could get a handhold. Daniel gritted his teeth so hard his jaw hurt.

The front door was only a few steps away. If he could endure a few more minutes of torture without breaking heads he'd get down on his knees in thanksgiving.

Suddenly Skylar balked. "Wait a minute. This is not the way to my dressing room."

"I know."

"Where are you taking me?"

"Out of here."

"No." She jerked loose, seething with outrage. "I'm not leaving with you."

Out of the corner of his eye, Daniel could see a beefy-looking man with tattoos on his arms and his hair swept upward into a pompadour heading their way. He looked like something that ought to be handling snakes at a two-bit carnival.

"You're going to get more than you bargained for if we don't leave. Now."

"What's the matter, preacher? Can't take the heat?"

"Come on, Sky. Please."

"No. You go ahead. I'm staying."

She whirled away from him, and though he called out to her it was futile. She rushed back into the crowd...and straight into the arms of the snake-handler.

"I got just what you lookin' for, dollbaby," he said.

In that instant everything Daniel had always believed about himself went up in smoke, leaving him to face the stark truth: Every man has his breaking point. Even Daniel.

He never knew how he reached Skylar so fast, but suddenly he was beside her, holding her around the waist so tightly he feared she might break in half, his other hand clenched into a fist at his side.

In readiness? To keep from punching the man's face?

Daniel hoped he never had to find out. He hoped to escape the potentially explosive situation.

"The lady is with me."

He hoped he sounded convincing and just edgy enough to break bones if he had to. It helped that he was tall and had the build of a football player, thanks to all that basketball and baseball he played with the church's youth group, plus a very good set of barbells in the basement of the parsonage.

"It don't look that way to me. In fact, 'pears to me the little lady has had a change of heart about you, Buster."

"No, she's with me."

"Well now, why don't we just ask the little lady," the man drawled, and Daniel braced himself for the worst.

Skylar wished she were anywhere in the world except slap dab in the middle of a horrible situation she'd created all by herself. She held her arms close to her sides to control her trembling.

What had she done? What had she been thinking?

Of course, it was obvious. She hadn't been thinking at all. She'd merely seen herself cornered and reacted. As she always did. And with disastrous results.

Well, not yet. But soon. She could see it coming. The flying fists, the punched-in faces, the bloody noses. The headlines.

Oh, Lord, the headlines…Daniel's name smeared all over the paper. The terrible consequences. His reputation ruined. His career over.

Why oh why hadn't she thought of that before she went barging off on her fool's mission? Why hadn't she simply done the sensible thing and written him a polite note saying, Please stay away from me. I'm not interested in you. I don't want you to call. I don't want you to drop by. I want you *gone*. Period.

Why hadn't she done that?

She felt something bitter in her mouth. The taste of fear and regret.

Daniel stood beside her like a rock, and in front of her was an evil apparition who looked more monster than man. Trouble in tattoos. Disaster in the making.

And only she could stop it.

But at what price?

Waiting for Skylar's answer, Daniel tensed every muscle in his body. His jaw ached, his head hurt, even his skin felt too tight.

"I'm with him," Skylar said, and it took Daniel a second to realize she meant *him*. When she turned, he saw the glisten of unshed tears in her eyes. "Take me out of here."

He would risk no more confrontations, no more narrow escapes, no more grabbing hands. With one swift move he picked Skylar up and carried her from the club.

It had turned cooler, fall coming to Mississippi at last, and the moon rode the sky like a galleon plowing through a sea of stars. Any other time Daniel would have stopped to appreciate the splendor of the heavens. Tonight he had only one thought in mind: getting Skylar out of harm's way.

Thankfully, she lay in his arms, acquiescent. Daniel didn't stop until he'd reached his car. Wouldn't it be wonderful if he didn't have to stop? Ever. Wouldn't it be great if he could keep Skylar in his arms? Wouldn't it be remarkable if he could keep on walking until they'd come to a place where two people could be completely safe and freed from the expectations of society, a secret paradise cut off from the rest of the world?

Still holding on to his precious bundle, he flexed his knees so he could reach the car door, then he set her on the front seat.

"Don't move."

He sprinted around the car, half expecting her to bolt, but when he got to the other side and slid behind the wheel, Skylar was sitting with her shoulders slumped, her head down, her long dark hair covering her face.

"Skylar?"

No answer. Daniel gently caressed her upper arm. Her skin felt cold to his touch. Reaction was setting in.

"Sky?"

She looked up at him, her eyes enormous and shimmering with internal grief, her face etched with the tragedy of her private hell.

"I'm sorry," she whispered. "For everything."

Now was not the time to ask questions. Now was not the time to pry for motives, push for answers. At the moment Skylar needed a friend, not a counselor.

"Hey, no problem. You rescued me and I rescued you right back."

That brought a hint of a smile to her face. He turned the key and started to drive with no destination in mind. Anywhere would do as long as it wasn't Babe's.

He drove along the high bluffs where the past whispered through the trees. He passed the antebellum mansions where General John C. Pemberton made the agonizing decision to surrender a city that had been known as the Gibraltar of the Confederacy, and where General Ulysses S. Grant slept for three days following the forty-seven-day siege of Vicksburg.

Far below him two mighty rivers converged, the Yazoo and the Mississippi. Tonight Daniel saw the rivers not as they were, lit by thousands of electric lights from the shops and restaurants and houses and gambling riverboats, but as they must have appeared to Newitt Vick when he first thought of founding a city on their banks. Pristine and beautiful. Nature's perfect highway where a man could load his cotton on a barge and go south all the way to New Orleans. Or north through Mark Twain country, all the way to Minnesota.

He felt a kinship with the city and with the vanished glory of its past. He wanted to turn to Skylar and say, Did you know that Vicksburg was founded by an itinerant

Methodist minister? A man defined not by his profession, but by his vision?

Instead, he drove in silence, drove until he saw out of the corner of his eye how Skylar sat taller, lifted her chin higher, tilted her head at a proud angle.

"Daniel, will you take me back to get my car now?"

"Yes."

He found a small graveled farm road almost hidden by trees that snaked off the highway toward the vast fields beyond. Daniel turned the car and headed back toward Babe's.

Skylar's car was the only one in the lot.

"I'll follow you home."

"No...please," she said, and then after he'd seen her safely to her car she held out her hand. "Thank you, Daniel."

Her hand was small-boned and graceful. Cradled between his own it felt fragile as the wings of a baby bird. Daniel held on longer than necessary, marveling at the power of touch to move a man to tears.

"Thank you," she whispered once more, and then she drove away.

He stood in the parking lot until her car had disappeared down the street. Then, honoring her request, he drove in the opposite direction, back to Belle Rose.

Chapter Seventeen

Skylar supposed she could hide in her parents' house with the faded slipcovers and the outdated draperies and the worn carpet, but that had never been her style. Besides, if she had any hope of launching a successful campaign to keep Daniel away, she had to go about her business as if nothing had happened, as if her outrageous performance at Babe's was an everyday occurrence.

And so she fed her cat, put on her tight black jeans and a bright red sweater that would raise eyebrows, then set off to the nursing home. As she approached she began to rehearse what she would say if she saw Daniel—something that would cement last night's impression of her in his mind.

"Hello, preacherman, nice buns." She made a face in the rearview mirror. Maybe she'd be more subtle. "Well, hello, preacher, I thought I'd come slumming again today."

She made a gagging sound. She couldn't denigrate her

nursing home visits even to help a worthy cause, i.e., saving
the Reverend Westmoreland from his own misguided intentions.

Tomorrow she'd probably think of a dozen clever retorts,
but for today she'd play the coward. That was it. Avoid
him. Even if it meant neglecting one of *her* patients.

The first thing she'd do after she'd parked her car and
gone inside would be to hurry down the hall toward Michael Westmoreland's room. Hoping the door would be
open. Hoping for a glimpse of Daniel. Hoping she could
pass by without any expression whatsoever on her face.

Hoping he wouldn't notice that she'd been crying.

Just as she entered the building, the janitor appeared
around the corner carrying a mop and a bucket.

"Lordy, Miss Skylar. What's the matter with you?"

There was no use lying to Bob. He had the eyes of an
eagle and the instincts of a mother hen. Ever since Skylar
had been singing for his wife, Bob had considered her a
part of his family.

"Nothing serious, Bob. I just had a good cry."

"Oh, is that all?" Relief flooded his face. "Lordy, I
remember when Harriet used to do that. Said it was good
for what ailed her." He propped on his mop handle, prepared to talk a spell. "And guess what? She was right.
After one of her crying fits she'd walk around the house
just a-smilin' as big as you please."

"I'm glad to hear that."

"So where's that smile, Miss Skylar?"

She gave him one. Otherwise she'd be there forever trying to convince Bob that she was all right.

Was she?

After last night's sorry performance in front of Daniel,
she might never be all right again.

So, what else is new?

Skylar hated that inner voice, that sarcastic, scathing little voice that reminded her of cringing in the back of the church while her daddy's hell-fire-and-damnation voice thundered around her.

"There, now, that's better," Bob said, then he patted Skylar's arm and she walked on down the hall.

Michael's door was standing wide open. Skylar braced herself, and when she came even with it she tilted her chin up and sailed past as fast as she could walk, all the while trying to catch a glimpse inside the room. Just in case...

Just in case Daniel was sitting beside his father's bed with his blond hair falling into his left eye. Just in case he glanced her way. Just in case he called her name.

Skylar's heart beat too fast, and her breath came in uneven spurts as if she'd just run the Boston Marathon and had come in second place in spite of putting forth a final burst of speed as she neared the finish line.

"Skylar?"

The voice was husky, but definitely female.

Skylar turned and found herself facing one of the most beautiful woman she'd ever seen. High cheekbones, hair black as shoe polish, enormous green eyes with an exotic tilt at the corner.

"You have to be Skylar." The woman held out her hand. "I'm Hannah, Daniel's sister."

Skylar could see it now, the strong bones, the finely chiseled features that spoke of ancestors with blue blood and a knack for careful selection of their gene pool. She'd bet there was not a single skeleton in the Westmoreland's family closet. Not a single black sheep. Not a whiff of scandal.

And certainly no one the family would be ashamed of. A con man or a thief or a star of the most explicitly sexual music video in America.

Why in the world was Hannah Westmoreland offering her hand to a woman like herself?

The smart thing to do would be to walk on down the hall. Add insult to injury. Disgust Daniel then snub his sister.

Skylar stuck out her hand. Nobody had ever accused her of being smart.

"Yes, I'm Skylar." Hannah's handshake was firm, her smile warm. "How did you know about me?"

Skylar wavered between hope that Daniel had told Hannah about her work with the nursing-home patients and the fear that he'd told her more.

"Daniel told me, and you're every bit as lovely as he said."

Was that all he'd said?

"Thank you."

"I was hoping you'd come today while I'm here with Dad alone. I wanted a chance to talk to you."

"Though I've been singing to the patients here for several years now, I'm afraid I can't give you any kind of professional opinion about your dad. All I do is try to give them music."

"Not about Dad. About Daniel."

"He's all right, isn't he?"

"Oh, my God. This is beautiful, *beautiful*."

"What? What are you talking about?"

"You. Daniel." Hannah chuckled. "You should have seen your face when I said I wanted to talk about my brother. Everything was there...concern, pleasure, love."

Oh help. This woman was nobody's fool. Skylar doubted that in Hannah's lifetime more than one or two people had ever gotten the best of her. Skylar wasn't even going to try.

Hannah gave her full-bodied laugh again. "I warn you,

though, I always say exactly what I think and I'm nosey
besides.''

''No warning necessary. It's obvious.''

''Which one?''

''Both.''

This time they both laughed, and suddenly Skylar saw
how easy it would be to attach herself to this lively,
straightforward woman. She missed female friendships. Not
that she didn't have any. There was Louise who'd been her
friend since they were in sixth grade together, but she'd
married right out of high school and moved to Chicago with
her husband. For a few years they'd written regularly and
never failed to call on birthdays and Christmas. And then
Louise had started having kids and Skylar had started driving her daddy crazy and the letters had decreased to one or
two a year and finally petered out altogether. The phone
calls had continued till Louise's husband had had his first
heart attack, then they'd dwindled to once in a blue moon.

Skylar had Pete's wife, but that was not the kind of close
friendship where she could walk in and kick off her shoes
and spill her heart all over their chipped walnut coffee table.

Then there were Kiki and Lulu from college, but Kiki
had never been one for small talk, and Lulu had abandoned
it altogether after she got into medical school.

All in all, Skylar had no one to talk to. Except her cat,
and Pussy Willow was too opinionated to be counted on in
a pinch.

Last night, for instance, she'd walked into Skylar's bedroom, taken one sniff at her mistress's tear-soaked pillow,
and huffed off to the kitchen with her nose in the air.

Because Chicago might as well be Mars, and whole con-
tinents separated Skylar from college pals, and her cat was
a fair-weather friend, she went into Michael Westmore-

land's room with Daniel's sister. She sat in a chair by the window and the sunshine warmed her face while she talked and talked.

And when Hannah asked her to sing she did that, too. Because she liked Hannah. Because she liked Michael.

And because she loved Daniel.

Chapter Eighteen

I hear singing. Who? I don't know this voice. Not my daughters. Not Anne. Am I hearing music from the other side? A siren's song designed to lure me into the Great Beyond?

It would be so easy to sink into the fog that surrounds me. To stop struggling.

I can't. I won't.

Too much to do. Em's getting married. To Jake. This much I know.

When? I can't remember. I have no way to account for time.

How long have I been in this deep hole, this eternal fog? A week? A month?

Lord God in heaven, let it not be longer. Don't leave Annie out there alone.

If I could only blink my eyes. So heavy...drifting again...fog closing in...

No! I've got to hold on.
The music…keep singing….don't stop…
Anne…I need you. Annie….

Chapter Nineteen

At first, Daniel thought he was dreaming, and then he realized he was hearing real voices. His mother and Clarice. Apparently going through his father's desk. Totally unaware that Daniel was stretched out on the sofa.

"I haven't been in Michael's office since he went into the coma," his mother said. "Since June. It seems like forever."

"I read somewhere about a woman who emerged from a coma after two years."

"Michael's not going to be in a coma for two years. I'm going to think of something to bring him back." Daniel was about to sit up when his mother added, "Daniel needs him as much as I do."

"Daniel? I would have said Emily."

"Well, of course, she especially wants him to be present for her wedding, but there's something bothering Daniel."

"Has he said anything?"

"No. You know him. He keeps everything inside, and besides he's trying so hard to be strong for the whole family. I can't put my finger on it, but something is troubling Daniel besides the obvious."

Now Daniel felt trapped. Not that his mother would feel embarrassed that she'd been talking about him for she would never say anything about him or any of her children that she wouldn't say to their faces. He was embarrassed on his own account.

He didn't want to be caught eavesdropping. Unintentional or not, that's what he was doing.

There was nothing for him now but to face the music. His mother and Clarice would probably laugh. Then they'd want to know why he was sleeping on the sofa in Michael's office.

And then he'd have to decide how much to tell them. Obviously he couldn't say, I had a disturbing encounter with Skylar at Babe's, and since I didn't have Dad to talk to I did the next best thing and slept in here surrounded by his things.

What would he say?

The teakettle saved him. It gave a piercing whistle and Clarice said, "Lord, that sounds good. I want plenty of sugar in mine."

The minute they were out the door, Daniel bolted off the sofa, fluffed up the pillow, refolded the afghan and raced into the downstairs bath to wash his face and comb his hair.

When he strolled into the kitchen, Clarice squinted at him over her teacup, and Anne said, "You look like you slept in your clothes."

"I did."

"Want some tea?"

"Thank you. That sounds good."

He sat down at the table facing the window so he could

feel the sun on his face, then nabbed a blueberry muffin. His favorite.

"Where are Emily and Jake?"

"Off on some mysterious wedding-planning errand. They didn't say what." She poured more tea into Daniel's cup. "Take your time. Hannah's with Dad."

It wasn't his father Daniel was thinking of, but Skylar. Of whether she'd gone to the nursing home. Of what she would wear, how she would look, how she would act.

Events of last night weighed heavily on his mind, and though he'd sat in the dark in his Dad's study for hours after he'd come home, he still had no answers.

To anything, actually.

Daniel felt as if he'd been cast into a wilderness without a map, without even a compass. With nothing to guide him except instinct, and lately his had deserted him.

"I know," he said. "I thought I'd go there any-how...unless you need me here."

Clarice spoke up. "Yep, we do. Anne and I are fixing to ransack this place, and we need some muscle."

Daniel laughed. "I can't remember when anybody has referred to me as 'some muscle.'"

Clarice laughed. "You ought to hear what they call you at the nursing home."

"I probably don't want to know."

But he did, of course. In case the *somebody* in question was Skylar Tate. In case she was saying good things about him in private that she didn't say to his face. Or couldn't. Lord, if he didn't get to the bottom of all this business he was going to go crazy.

"Down there at Tranquility Manor they call you, 'That Preacher, the Hunk.'"

"Who?" Daniel had to know.

"You're not going to believe this. It's that dour-looking Sally Schuster."

Anne was quick to defend the underdog. "She's been wonderfully kind to us. Anyway, she can't help the way she looks."

"Lord, Anne, don't get on your high horse with me…she could *smile.*" Clarice set her teacup on the table and stood up. "Let's get cracking or we'll never find Michael's diaries."

"You're looking for Dad's diaries?"

"Yes, the early ones. I found his last journal this morning when I finally unpacked his gear."

Guilt slashed Daniel. She was talking about the gear Michael had carried with him on that fateful trip to the Himalayas. Why hadn't Daniel already done that? Or one of his sisters?

"I should have done that for you."

"You didn't think of it…and quite frankly, neither did I. It's done. That's all that counts. Now let's go and see if we can find Michael's diaries."

"We don't have to search. I know where they are."

"Michael told you?"

"No. I found them when I was ten. Actually, Hannah and I both found them."

"Where?"

"In the attic. You know how we used to go up there on rainy days…I guess we explored every inch of that attic. They're in that old rolltop desk underneath the skylight. At least, they were twenty years ago."

Anne sat down at the kitchen table as if her legs wouldn't hold her.

"I should have guessed. Michael always loved to go up there. 'Puttering around' is what he always said."

When Anne put her hands to her cheeks, Daniel could see them shaking. In fact, his mother looked pale.

"If they're going to upset you, maybe you shouldn't read them."

"Oh, I *must*. Don't you see, except for memories that's the only way I can still hear his voice."

"I'll get them for you."

"No. Wait. I think I want to go up there and read them."

"I'll go with you, Anne."

"No, Clarice. I need to do it this way. By myself."

With that, Anne started up the stairs and Clarice grabbed Daniel's arm.

"Talk to her, Daniel. She's so damned stubborn I don't know how any of us can put up with her."

Anne turned around and said, "May the bird of paradise fly up your nose, Clarice," then both of them broke up laughing. Anne laughed so hard she had to hold on to the banister to keep from falling, and Daniel feared she was nearing hysteria.

Then suddenly she smiled at them and said, "I'm all right. I'm going to be all right."

Clarice waited until she was out of earshot then she tugged Daniel back into the kitchen and began rummaging in the cabinets till she found what she wanted—a very good merlot.

"Where's the corkscrew?"

Daniel wasn't about to say anything about having a glass of wine in the middle of the morning, not after all his she-nanigans of the last few days.

"I'll get it." He opened the bottle and Clarice poured herself a glass. "Want some?" she asked, and when he shook his head, she said, "You could probably use it. Dealing with Skylar Tate is not easy."

Daniel plopped into his chair as if he'd been gut-punched. "Do you send out spies or are you clairvoyant?"

His mother's friend laughed. "Lord, Daniel, I've been keeping my finger on the pulse of this town since I was thirty-five." She took a sip of her wine then grinned and added, "Better make that sixteen, 'cause I'm only thirty-six now."

Clarice topped off her glass, then handed him the bottle. "Put that in the fridge before I make a fool of myself, then you get out of here and see if you can't find Skylar Tate."

"Mom's probably going to need me after she finishes reading the diaries."

"No, she's gonna need *me*. I'll cry with her and rant and rave and carry on and maybe get just a little bit drunk, then we'll both feel better, and afterward we'll take a long walk in the woods and sit down there on that old petrified log that overlooks the river and she can say any damned thing she wants to me." She grinned at him. "Stuff she would never tell her son."

"You're a jewel…"

Clarice held up her hand to stop him. "Don't say any more," she said. "I might have to try and live up to it. Go on, take care of what's been bothering you so your momma can get some peace."

He kissed her on the cheek, and Clarice shooed him out the door. Daniel didn't need much urging. In less than fifteen minutes he'd showered, changed into fresh clothes and was on his way to the nursing home. Beard be damned.

"She's gone," Hannah said the minute Daniel walked into his father's room. Daniel didn't even try to pretend ignorance, not with his older sister who had eyes in the back of her head, X-ray vision and mind-reading ability. That's what she used to tell him and Emily to keep them in line. Hannah had always relished her role as oldest of the Westmoreland siblings.

Daniel sank into a chair. "You saw her?"

"Not only saw her, but talked to her for a very long time." She grinned. "I really, really like this girl, Daniel, and so does Dad." She patted Michael's hand. "Don't you, Dad?"

"You didn't grill her the way you did poor Jake, did you, Hannah?"

Hannah hooted with laughter. "Skylar Tate wouldn't put up with my high-handed tactics for a second. Trust me, Daniel, this woman is pure gold, and if you intend to marry her you'd better get your butt out of here and batter at her door till she lets you in."

"Who said anything about marrying her?"

"Don't you think I know you, Daniel? Love's written all over both your faces, and you're not the kind to embark on an affair. You and Emily are just alike, traditional to the bone. Not a thing like me. Sometimes I think both of you are adopted."

Daniel laughed. "You're the maverick, Hannah. A foundling left on the doorstep. Right, Dad?"

Hannah threw a copy of *Daily Devotionals* left in the room by a cadre of Baptists who visited every fifth Sunday. "Get out of here before you really get in trouble. Go find Skylar and strike while the iron is hot."

"What do you mean?"

"Not what your red face is telling me, bro. I'm talking about Miss Skylar Tate. I've got her primed for love."

"Hannah...what have you been telling her about me?"

"Good stuff...mostly." She waved her hand toward the door. "Go on. I've got things covered here."

"Thanks, sis."

"Don't call me sis," Hannah yelled as he left the room.
"You know how I hate that."

Daniel was smiling when he left the nursing home because suddenly everything seemed simple to him. Two people loved each other, therefore they should be together. He didn't even question Hannah's judgment. She was the least sentimental person he knew. If she said she saw love in Skylar's face, then she saw love. Period.

As he got into his car and drove toward Skylar's house, Daniel's only regret was that his father might never know about her. He might never know that at long last his only son had found the magic he'd witnessed between his parents his entire life.

Now all Daniel had to do was convince Skylar.

Chapter Twenty

W hen Skylar walked into her house the curtains struck her all of a sudden as a symbol of everything that was wrong in her life, and she couldn't stand them a minute longer. She raced to her windows and started ripping them off the walls. Pussy Willow jumped off the sofa where she'd been napping and scampered under the TV.

Ordinarily Skylar would have apologized to her cat. She'd have said, "Sorry, Pussy W., this is nothing personal." But today she was too distraught. There was too much on her mind. The past crowded in trying to smother her and the future was hammering so hard she could barely think.

She didn't stop until every window was stripped bare, then she sank into the heap of tattered curtains in the middle of her living-room floor and closed her eyes, overwhelmed.

Her conversation with Hannah drifted through her mind, word for word. "All my life I've been looking for a safe harbor,'' she'd told Hannah, she who had never in her life confessed anything to anybody. Skylar had always kept her true feelings inside. It was the only way she could escape recriminations.

''Where did you look?'' Hannah asked.

''Paris, Rome, the Greek Islands. I was like some kind of migratory bird, alighting in one foreign port after the other always hoping to find a haven.''

''And did you?''

''No. Nothing ever satisfied. Nothing felt right. When I left I'd be filled with the same restlessness that had brought me there in the first place.

''Your safe harbor is not a place, Skylar,'' Hannah told her. ''It's a person, and I think you already know who he is.''

Skylar did, but until she said it aloud she could still pretend it wasn't so.

''You're safe with Daniel,'' Hannah had said.

And now Skylar couldn't get the words out of her head. Dust from the curtains made her sneeze, and Pussy Willow came to sit beside her on the untidy heap of faded and torn fabric, and still Skylar could think of nothing except the one man who was the best thing that had ever happened to her…and the worst.

She would never in a million years fit into his fishbowl world. She covered her face with her hands trying to shut out the thoughts.

''Skylar…'' There was Daniel framed in her doorway. ''The door was open.''

''I thought I'd never see you again.''

''Is that what you want?''

Time suspended as they stared at each other across the space, and Skylar knew in her bones that every dream, every hope she'd ever had depended on how she answered Daniel's question.

"No..." The minute the word was out of her mouth, he moved toward her. "That's not what I want...I..."

He knelt beside her and stopped her words with a kiss that reeled them both over backward until they were tangled together in the curtains. Dust billowed around them...and hope. Such hope that Skylar's heart caught fire and she glowed with the wonderful possibility that had eluded her all her life.

Daniel had come to her in spite of all her efforts at driving him away, and if she denied him now she might never get another chance at happiness. She wrapped her arms tighter and pulled him so close she could feel the beating of his heart against her own.

"Last night I was afraid I'd lost you," she whispered.

"You'll never lose me, Skylar."

"Oh, Daniel, I don't deserve..."

"Shhh." He put his hand over her lips and she kissed his fingertip. "Magic just happens."

He captured her once more—her lips, her arms, her legs so that she was cocooned against him and safe. So very safe.

"I wish we could stay like this forever," she said, and Daniel brushed his fingertips tenderly along the side of her jaw and told her, "We can."

They didn't say anything else for a long while, content instead to lie side by side drinking each other in, absorbing each other through their eyes, their skin, their hearts. It was the most romantic moment Skylar had ever known. In fact, it was the *only* romantic moment she'd ever known.

The men who had passed through her life had merely skimmed the surface, never delving deep enough to know her, never taking the time to try to please her, and never,

never touching her heart. It suddenly occurred to her that the chance of two true lovers finding each other in the vastness of the universe was small indeed, and if she turned her back on this miracle she was spitting in the face of fate.

Oh, she had no doubt she could find someone else, but she would never, *never* find another soul mate. She would never find another person who filled her heart and created magic the way Daniel Westmoreland did.

Daniel felt like a sixteen-year-old. Here he was lolling around on dusty old curtains in the middle of Skylar Tate's floor, and he felt as if he were in the most romantic spot in the world. Candlelight and roses couldn't have made things any better. A full moon and a night sky full of stars. A sunset over a painted sea. Nothing could have topped the moment.

He memorized her face with his eyes, his fingertips, while everything he'd meant to say fled his mind. Things such as "Let's go out to dinner and see if we can't reclaim our common ground," or "Let's take a walk down by the river and talk," or "Let's start all over and see what happens." There was only one thing to say to this woman. One thing to do.

"Skylar, will you marry me?"

"Yes."

If she'd hesitated Daniel might have backtracked and added, "As soon as Emily's wedding is over and I've settled things at the nursing home for Mom." But she'd accepted him in the wink of an eye, and suddenly nothing else mattered. They had this enormous love that had already overcome tremendous odds. What could possibly go wrong that the two of them couldn't fix? Together.

Chapter Twenty-One

From the diary of Anne Beaufort Westmoreland:

September 24, 2001

It's quiet here at the nursing home, but then it always is this time of night. The evening rounds finished, the last dose of medicine dispensed, everybody sleeping except the nurse on the night shift and me.

I can't sleep. I'm too excited, still reeling from Daniel's news. He's getting married. Even as I write these words I can still hardly believe it. Oh, don't get me wrong. I love the girl. I really do, and he looks happier than I've ever seen him.

Skylar Tate. A Huntsville girl. Southern to the bone. I like that.

He brought her by early this evening right before

Hannah left for Belle Rose, and she didn't even act surprised. I haven't been kept deliberately in the dark...my children wouldn't do that. It's just that I've been preoccupied with Michael and Daniel only just met Skylar. Here at Tranquility Manor of all places.

Still...I knew the minute I saw Michael that I would marry him. True love socks you right in the heart. Let others court for months and even years. Soul mates simply *know*.

Oh, and I do believe Daniel and Skylar are soul mates. Not that my opinion matters. Lord, I remember how Mother tried to talk me out of loving Michael. As if anybody could. As if anything short of a cataclysmic end-of-time event could keep the two of us apart. And not even then, for Michael and I are destined to be together always, in this lifetime and beyond.

Well, anyhow...Daniel and Skylar had already gone to apply for their license. Hannah laughed heartily at that. "Striking while the iron is hot," she called it, and then she and Daniel grinned at each other as if they knew something the rest of us didn't.

I'll have to ask her about that tomorrow. Seems she and Skylar had already met, and I'm happy to say the two of them carried on together as if they were bosom buddies. That's so wonderful to see. I would hate any divisiveness in this family.

Lord, I'll never forget when Emily announced she was marrying Jake how Hannah carried on. She came around though. That good Westmoreland blood.

"I hope Emily won't think we're stealing her thunder," Skylar told us, and I said, "No, of course not." That's when she told me that she and Daniel aren't going to have a church wedding anyhow, but are going to have a private and very simple ceremony. With their own vows. Well, that certainly took me by surprise, Daniel being a minister and all, but I didn't say anything.

I guess that's what being a good mother-in-law is all about. Not saying anything. At least that's what Clarice said when I called to tell her about Daniel and Skylar. She has two daughters-in-law, and to hear her tell it they both think she walks on water.

Lord, that Clarice...what would I do without her? When I broke apart and cried right in the middle of telling her all that happy news she said, "That's all right, Anne. I understand your sadness."

And she does, for Clarice sees with her heart. She knows that seeing two of my children marry is bittersweet for me because Michael is not here to share it all. Oh, Daniel told him. I don't mean that. He stood right there by that bed and held his father's hand. "Dad," he said, "I'm marrying the most beautiful woman in the world, somebody you already know. Remember how she sang for you, Dad? Well, now you'll get to hear that angel's voice anytime you want."

Hannah and I both cried when he said that. Skylar too.

Well, enough of all these weepy confessions. I'm sick and tired of crying. I want to get on with living.

And I want Michael there at my side. Not lying here in this nursing home like a turnip.

As soon as I finish this entry I'm going to crawl into that bed and act as if we're home in Belle Rose. I'm going to slither under the covers and do no telling what to him. I swear I am. Surely when I touch him he knows. Surely he's stirred in the depths of his soul.

That's what he used to always tell me. "Anne, you stir my soul."

When is he going to wake up and tell me that again?

Lord, if I didn't have his diaries now I think I'd go crazy.

Reading them is like hearing his voice. All those quotations he collected over the years, the little bits of wisdom he gleaned from other sources, the things he found noteworthy.

And oh, the lovely things he said about me, about us. I thumb through his diaries, his letters to me and the memories are balm to my soul.

I think I'll read some more before I climb into bed with him. He seems so far away now. Unreachable, almost. But he'll come back to me. I know he will. Because I love him. Because he loves me. I need to read the things he wrote so we won't lose that heart-connection.

Chapter Twenty-Two

From the diary of Michael Westmoreland:

October 13, 1966

"Better to be without logic than without feeling." Charlotte Brontë wrote those words and today I found out what she meant, for today I met the love of my life, the woman of my dreams, the woman I intend to marry. Come hell or high water.

When I walked into that bus station this afternoon and saw Anne Beaufort sitting in the sunshine reading, my heart flew to hers without a moment's hesitation, circumstances be damned. Being with her tonight at the Algonquin merely confirmed my feeling: This woman and I were destined to meet, destined to be together. For all time.

If I deny that I might as well cut off my right arm and anesthetize my heart, for she's the only woman I can ever feel truly alive with. This I know.

Getting together is not going to be easy. God, how I wish it were. How I wish I'd never met Sarah, never been boxed into confessing a love I never really felt. How I wish I had never given her a ring.

Old Oscar Wilde told the truth when he said, "Suffering is a revelation. One discovers things never discovered before."

I have to break the engagement. There's no other way, for now I know that a marriage without true love will kill the spirit and deaden the heart. If I stay with Sarah after having met Anne I'll shackle some part of me that was meant to soar. Not only that, but Sarah will be denied the pleasure of being all she can truly be. She won't get the chance to grow, to spread her wings and fly, too.

It's not going to be easy. Telling either of them. Knowing Anne as I do (I've only been with her hours, and yet already I feel as if I know her to the bone), she'll take it all in stride, but Sarah will be a different matter. She'll try to chain me to her side with guilt. And reminders of a shared history, a commitment. Lord God, how I hate that word. Only the Puritans could have come up with something so soulless and cold. What the hell does it mean? Chained side by side, no matter what? All because of laws laid down by a bunch of men who knew everything about sin and nothing about joy.

True love needs no extrapolation. Only true love truly binds. And without a bunch of sanctified, sanctimonious old farts carping about commitment and making folks pledge until death do us part.

Hell, death can't part true lovers. Both Anne and I know that.

When I marry that woman...and I *will* marry her...we'll write our own vows. We'll speak love and leave the words of bondage to people less aware.

Chapter Twenty-Three

Skylar was in the midst of writing the vows she would say to Daniel when she panicked. Tomorrow she was supposed to stand on the bluff overlooking the Mississippi and pledge herself to Daniel in front of his family. She, Skylar Tate, married to a preacher!

She must be going crazy. That was it. Living out of a suitcase for years and having conversations with a cat had driven her over the brink. Why else would she be setting herself up for a future doomed to failure?

She would run away. Pack her bag and catch the first bus out of Vicksburg.

Grabbing a suitcase from the top of her closet, Skylar began to toss in clothes. She was good at this. She'd done it many, many times.

Pussy Willow jumped on the bed and nosed around the wadded clothes, then sniffed in disgust and walked off.

"It's for the best P.W., you'll see. Someday Daniel will

thank me.'' Skylar tossed her perfume on top of a pair of silk pajamas, and all of a sudden she thought about Daniel, standing underneath the ancient oak waiting for her. Daniel who had never been anything except wonderful.

She picked up the phone and dialed his number. ''Daniel?'' He made a few sleepy sounds into the receiver and only then did she look at the clock. ''Oh lord, I'm sorry. I didn't know what time it is. Go back to sleep.''

''Sky? What's wrong?''

''Everything. I can't do this, Daniel. I can't marry you.''

''I'm coming over.''

''No...Daniel...wait. It's three o'clock in the morning.''

''Stay right where you are. Don't you go anywhere, Sky. Promise you won't leave.''

''Please don't come, Daniel. I'm no good for you.''

''Say it, Sky! Say you'll wait for me. Please...''

She sighed. ''All right. But it won't do any good. I've already made up my mind.''

''We'll talk...as long as you like...and if you still feel the same way after that, then you can leave.''

''You won't try to stop me?''

''No, I won't try to stop you.''

''All right, then.''

Daniel broke speed limits. If the cops stopped him he'd have to go to jail without a shirt or socks. Beard stubble and bleary eyes.

He let off the accelerator. He couldn't go to jail. He had to see Skylar. He had to talk her out of leaving him.

When he pulled up she was standing at the door, and he bolted from the car so fast that he left his car door wide open. All the way over he'd worried about what to say to her, what to do. Give her space or hug her close? Start the conversation or wait and listen?

Now there was no hesitation. None whatsoever. He scooped her into his arms and pressed her close, cradling her head with one hand and stroking her back with the other.

"Daniel…"

"Shhh. Just let me hold you a while."

Sighing, she swayed against him, and they stood that way for a long while, gently moving back and forth like two saplings in a summer wind.

"This feels wonderful," she murmured against his chest.

He said, "Hmmm," and kept on rocking her, rocking her gently in his love.

Leaning back slightly so she could see his face she said, "You don't know me at all."

"I know everything I need to know, Sky. You have a loving and generous heart."

"I can never fit in. I can never be a proper preacher's wife. I can never act pious and pretend to be something I'm not."

"You don't have to pretend. I love you exactly the way you are, and I don't want you to change. Not for me, not for anybody. Didn't I tell you that already?"

"Yes."

"You won't have to fill a role. You won't have to meet anybody's expectations. You can continue your career or not. It's up to you."

She shook her head as if she couldn't believe it, then burrowed closer to his chest. "Oh, Daniel…."

"What? Tell me what else is bothering you, Sky."

"I'm scared. I've never had anything this wonderful. I've never known what it was like to love and be loved in this absolutely accepting, totally encompassing way and I'm afraid if I blink my eyes it'll all be taken away. I would die if I lost you, Daniel."

In his profession Daniel had comforted many a bride-to-be with wedding-day jitters, but there was no way he could pass off what Skylar was feeling as a simple case of jitters. Her hurts were deep and wide, going back many years to a childhood without love.

And he couldn't make promises he might never be able to keep. Fate has a way of making liars of us all. Look what had happened to his dad. His father had surely never planned to leave his mother in that way, and yet there they were, two people deeply in love, separated by an event totally beyond their control.

Where was wisdom when Daniel needed it? Where was faith?

Soft light flooded around them, the silvery gleam of a full moon and the glow of stars shining unhampered into a room stripped bare of curtains. And all of sudden Daniel thought of Job, of how he'd railed against God for all his misfortunes. His answer had not been a pat on the head and the reassurance that all his petty strivings would come to fruition and his daily petitions be granted. No. His answer had been ''Where were you when I hung the moon and set the stars in place? Have you ever given orders to the morning or shown the dawn its place? Who are you to question?''

And Daniel saw how he had been his own undoing, how what he'd believed to be his unshakable faith had actually been his own arrogance...for thinking he had all the answers. He was merely a speck in the universe, a tiny blip on the cosmic screen.

He knew nothing...and yet what he knew was sufficient for the day. He knew that the heart is the surest guide to life. His dad, who had been a student of all the great philosophers and had collected their wisdom through the years, often quoted Pascal: ''The heart has its reasons of which reason knows nothing.'' And what was that wisdom of the heart except angels whispering to us the great cosmic truths?

The trick was to listen.

Daniel had been talking too much. It was time to start listening.

''I don't know what the future holds, Sky...for any of us. All I know is that a future without you would be too bleak to contemplate. Sometimes great love comes with great heartache. Look at Mom and Dad.''

''Oh, Daniel...I'm sorry. I didn't think.''

''If I called Mom and asked her whether she'd make the same choice if she'd known the outcome, what do you think she'd say?''

''I don't know her that well but from what I've seen, I'd say her answer would be yes.''

''That's the choice I make, Skylar. To take the risk, to love you with my whole heart no matter what the outcome. What is your choice?''

Her answer would consign him to heaven or to hell. He kept his arms around her while he waited for her answer, holding her loosely so she would be free to come or to go.

''My answer is yes, Daniel.'' A smile lit her face. ''Yes!''

Daniel kissed her softly, then let her go. ''I'll see you soon, darling. We have a date at the river at sunset.''

In that quiet time just before evening when the sun was low in the west, painting the sky and the river with gold, Daniel stood underneath a live oak tree high on a bluff and married the woman of his dreams. She came to him in white, not a traditional wedding gown but something soft and simple that floated around her when she walked toward him.

She wore a garland in her hair and smelled of gardenias. And when she put her hand into his and smiled, Daniel knew she loved him truly.

His family had gathered there on the bluff to witness his joy—Emily holding hands with Jake, Hannah giving the victory sign, and his mother with a smile on her face and her head held high. And though his father still slept the deep troubled sleep, there was a strong sweet spirit hovering around Anne that could only be Michael.

With his friend and fellow-minister there to make it official, Daniel said his vows to Skylar. And when it was her turn to speak, she took his breath away.

"With joy and thankfulness I give myself to you, heart, soul and mind. I pledge that I shall always love you truly all our days here on earth and beyond...throughout time eternal, until our love is perfected and we ascend to the heavens to become stars, binary and bright, ever circling in each other's orbit."

Chapter Twenty-Four

From the diary of Anne Beaufort Westmoreland:

September 27, 2001

They had to unlock the doors of the nursing home to let me in. Fortunately the director was very understanding about it. He said, "Mrs. Westmoreland, it's not every day a son gets married."

I would have come back whether they'd liked it or not. If they hadn't unlocked the doors I'd have climbed through the window because that's how I am. Indomitable. Just ask Michael.

I know, I know. I have to stop that. I have to stop thinking of Michael as the person I always turn to, the one I run to when I'm hurting or sad or lonely, but most of all the one I race to when I want to laugh and talk about everything under the sun and make wonderful, remarkable love until both our eyes pop out.

I told him all about the wedding after I got back, and I didn't leave out a thing. Not even the reception at Babe's. Michael would have laughed his head off at that one. In fact he'd have enjoyed everything about this wedding, including the fact that it wasn't held in a church. Mountains have always been Michael's cathedral. He used to tell me how he felt when he'd reached a summit, the sense of awe that stole over him, the wonder.

Sometimes I think that if I could get him back to the top of a mountain he'd be all right. He'd wake up and say, "I don't know what took me so long, darling."

Anyhow...back to the reception. Skylar's friend Pete and his wife put on what they called a shindig with barbecue and plenty of beer and lots of good Southern hospitality. He had a band and everything, and when Skylar took the stage and sang love songs to Daniel, she brought the house down. Clarice had a blast. Danced every dance. Most of them with a director from LA who just happened to be in town scouting locations for a new film. (Lord, I hope it's not going to be one of those dreary movies that make the South look like something out of Tobacco Row.)

I said to her, "Clarice, don't you even think of marrying again until Michael comes back." Of course, you know what she said, "Anne, marriage is not what I have on my mind." Then she rolled her eyes and smacked her lips and wiggled her hips. Typical, delightful Clarice. Somebody in charge should have cloned her.

I had a good time, which surprised me. I told Michael so. I said, "Darling, you'd better wake up soon or you're going to miss all the fun." I even told him about the new lawyer in town who flirted with me. I said, "Listen here, my love, I can still turn heads so you'd better hurry up and come back to me or else somebody else is liable to snatch me up and run."

Not that I would go. Not that I would ever leave my Michael. And certainly not that I would or could ever love anyone else.

There is only one man for me and that's my Michael. But just suppose complacency is not what he needs right now. What if a little worry might shake him out of his deep sleep? I'll try anything to have him back in my arms once more.

He looks so peaceful lying there in the moonlight. Almost as if he's dreaming sweet dreams. And maybe he is. Maybe he's dreaming about Daniel and Skylar honeymooning at Belle Rose. (Emily and Jake left for Atlanta right after the reception, said they had some things to take care of there before their wedding. And Hannah's staying with Clarice so Daniel and Skylar can have the house all to themselves.) Maybe Michael is remembering the day we bought Belle Rose, how he said we'd have to christen every room, how he carried me over the threshold the day we moved in although we'd been married six years. Six years or sixty. With Michael every day was a honeymoon.

Lord, I remember how long it took us to christen every room—years, what with Michael's being off on a mountain and me having the children. After they came it made our project harder. But in some ways more fun. Lord, we giggled like teenagers when we'd sneak into the bathroom in the middle of the day and lock ourselves in so the children wouldn't walk in on us. And when things really heated up as they always do between us, Michael would cover my mouth so the children wouldn't hear.

I've always been a noisy lover. That's one of the things Michael loved about me.

Loves. He still loves me. I know he does although he can no longer take me in his arms and tell me so. I have to believe that or else I'll go mad.

I have to believe he'll come back to me.

Chapter Twenty-Five

When Daniel had asked Skylar where she wanted to go on their honeymoon, she'd said, "Anywhere with you," and that's how they'd ended up at Belle Rose. For a number of reasons. It was one of the most romantic settings Daniel could think of, and it was nearby.

As he drove the three miles from Babe's he knew he'd chosen wisely. In his present condition, he'd have failed the endurance test of a drive across the country or a long plane ride. Skylar was his wife and he wanted to know her in the biblical sense. Old-fashioned, but true.

She was so quiet. He squeezed her hand. "What are you thinking, Sky?"

"I'm thinking about the reception."

He laughed. "It was fun, wasn't it?"

"Yes. But so much more. Letting me have it at a night-club was the most generous thing you could have done for me. It showed that you were totally honest when you told me I don't have to change a thing...thank you, Daniel.''

''It was my pleasure.'' He was glad she'd recognized the reception as symbolic, glad she'd told him, but now he wanted to move forward, not look backward. ''There is one thing I want you to change, though.''

''You can't be serious?''

He loved that about her, that she faced challenges head-on, spitting bullets and shooting fire.

''Oh, I'm dead serious.''

''Let's hear it, then.''

''I want you to change clothes.''

She laughed so hard she had to wipe tears from her eyes. Then suddenly, Belle Rose was in sight, rising up out of the moonlight in magnificent splendor, a place steeped in the past, a place strong enough to withstand a war and still provide shelter to generations. A place of endings and beginnings. A place of love.

''Welcome home, Mrs. Westmoreland.''

''Pinch me. I must be dreaming.''

''Oh, I plan to do more than that. Much, much more,'' he said, then he lifted her from the car and carried her over the threshold.

Hannah had made sure the lights were burning, then she'd picked roses putting on their last hoorah from the garden and arranged them in vases all over the house. The Zephrine Drouhin with its spicy sweet fragrance perfumed the entire downstairs and followed Daniel all the way up the staircase.

''You can't mean to carry me up all these flights of stairs,'' Skylar said, but he could tell she was pleased.

''Watch me.''

''I think I've married a virile man.'' She nuzzled his

neck. "Of course, it's too early to tell yet. Not without further proof."

"Can you wait till we get to the landing?"

"Hmmm…maybe."

Daniel laughed for sheer joy. This is what love should be—the easy banter, the quick laughter, the fun. "I don't know why I didn't do this sooner," he said, and Skylar's laughter pealed through the antebellum house.

"Let's see," she said. "We've known each other nine days. I don't think you could have done this much sooner."

"I'd have married you the day I met you."

"And I'd have said yes."

He pushed open his door and spread his bride upon the bed, and there, surrounded by the scent of roses and the glow of candlelight, Daniel made Skylar his own.

So this is love, Skylar thought.

Everything that had gone before paled by comparison. This was magic, pure and simple, and she'd known from the minute Daniel entered her. When she thought about it, they were practically strangers, and yet Skylar felt as if she'd known him always, not just in this life but in all the lives that had gone before.

He was heart of her heart, bone of her bone, soul of her soul. They were completely natural together, nothing held back, nothing taboo, just two people who were meant to be together loving each other.

For hours.…

Afterward, Daniel settled her down with caresses that felt like silk, then tucked her arms and legs into all the perfect places and drifted off in midsentence. One minute he was saying, "I love you, Sky…" and the next he was fast asleep.

Skylar watched him sleep because she didn't want to

miss a thing. She didn't want to miss a single moment of being with Daniel. He slept deeply and peacefully, a half smile on his lips.

"I love you, Daniel," she whispered and kissed him softly on the lips, but he didn't stir. Not even when she felt a cramp in her leg and had to shift position. The sleep of innocence, she thought and then smiled.

They'd left the French doors open because the weather was still mild, almost like summer, and the night breeze that drifted through was balmy and heavily perfumed with roses. Skylar gently untangled herself from Daniel and went to the balcony. The gardens of Belle Rose looked ethereal in the moonlight, thousands of sweetly scented blossoms underplanted with fragrant lavender and cascading over the marble arms and legs and faces of Greek statues. There was Hebe who bore cups to the gods, Athena whose wisdom was legendary and Venus the goddess of love.

Skylar leaned over the balcony breathing in the scented night, and suddenly arms slid around her from behind.

"What's the matter, darling? Couldn't sleep?"

"Hmmm." She leaned back into the curve of his arm. "It seemed such a waste of time."

"So it is." He kissed the back of her neck, sending delicious shivers all over her, and she turned into him, kissing him with a fervor that was contagious. They kissed until kissing was not enough.

"Here?" he whispered.

"Yes," she murmured as he lifted her gown, and then, anchoring herself to the balcony railing, she said it again, over and over, "yes, yes, yes, *yes*."

Afterward he picked her up and carried her back to the bed where she fell into a deep and dreamless sleep safe in the haven of her husband's arms.

* * *

Skylar woke slowly, stretching like her cat, and when she felt herself in an empty bed she sat up alarmed. Daniel laughed.

"I'm here, my love."

And so he was…standing in the doorway holding a silver tray and wearing nothing except a big grin. "I thought you might like breakfast in bed," he said, and she held her arms wide open.

"As long as you're the main course."

"I'm afraid you're mistaken, Mrs. Westmoreland. *You're* the main course."

He set the tray on the bedside table, then burrowed under the sheets and proved his point.

Her delight was noisy and prolonged, then afterward she lay against the pillows sighing. "I really love the way you think," she said, and he leaned over her laughing, then popped a fresh strawberry into her mouth.

"Eat up, my love. You're going to need your strength."

"Is that a promise?"

"It's a promise."

She opened her mouth for another strawberry, but he had other things in mind, delicious things, as a matter of fact, things that lasted the better part of the morning. When they finally surfaced, laughing and sated and wearing strawberry juice and remnants of chocolate and cream, she gave her new husband an arch grin.

"I hope this place has a bath."

"It does. Big enough for two." He scooped her up and set her in an enormous tub then crawled in behind her. "Ahh. Just right."

"Don't you think we're missing something?"

"What?"

"Water."

"Oh, that." He turned on the faucets, adjusted the temperature, then added bubble bath. As the bubbles rose to the tips of her breasts, he said, "I've always wanted to frolic in bubbles with a sexy woman."

"Any sexy woman?"

"No. It had to be you."

"I know that tune," Skylar said. Then she grabbed a bar of soap and holding it like a microphone, began to croon the love song to Daniel, meaning it with her whole heart.

Chapter Twenty-Six

From the diary of Anne Beaufort Westmoreland:

September 30, 2001

It has been three days since the wedding and as Mother said when she dropped by to visit Michael yesterday, "Nobody's seen hide nor hair of Daniel and Skylar."

She's still miffed that she didn't get to come to the wedding, but I had to remind her three times that she was sick, and besides that, Daniel and Skylar didn't have a big church wedding. Frankly we were all relieved that she couldn't come. That way we didn't have to tell her the reception was at Babe's.

Oh, I know, I know, that was cowardly, but the older Mother gets, the more judgmental she becomes. I can just picture the ruckus she'd have made over a member

f her family (particularly Daniel!) having a wedding
eception in a nightclub with a big neon sign of naked
irls that lights up the whole parking lot.

Clarice was delighted, of course. When she first saw
he sign she laughed so hard she had to hang on to the
ide of the car. Then she said, "Blue neon nudes with
ink neon tits. I love it!"

That's Clarice for you. Totally outrageous. Michael
lways got such a kick out of her company.

When she came to visit yesterday she brought a brass
orn with one of those big red bulbs on the end. "Like
Harpo Marx used," she said. Then she laid it on the
ed beside Michael's hand and said, "Since you won't
et your butt up from there and talk to us, why don't
ou just toot this every now and then to let us know
what you're thinking. Once if you agree with what we're
aying, and twice if you don't."

Then she picked up his hand and put it right over the
ubber bulb and sat back down and commenced to talk-
ng, as my mother would say. She pretends not to like
Clarice, but I know that she does. Why else would she
ave gone to Clarice's defense when the whole town
alked about how she'd married her second husband be-
ore her first was cold in the ground?

Anyhow, back to the horn...Clarice was saying, "I'll
et you if Michael had been at that wedding he'd have
ulled Daniel aside and said, 'Son, don't you ever let
anything come before your wife. Not even your chil-
ren.'"

And I swear I saw Michael's hand quiver as if he were
trying desperately to toot the horn. Once, I'm sure. Michael always put me first. As I did with him.

I believe that's why our marriage stayed as fresh as
if we'd become husband and wife only yesterday.

Clarice was right. I know that's what Michael woul
have told Daniel.

I'll have to remember to tell him myself. I'll probabl
see him this weekend. He asked for three days at Bell
Rose, but I told him to take a week. I stay here wit
Michael every night anyhow, and Clarice says she'
happy for my company at lunch every day. I think she'
enjoying Hannah's company, too. Clarice has bee
rather lonely since her daughter moved to California
though she'd stick pins under her fingernails befor
she'd ever admit it.

Chapter Twenty-Seven

Skylar decided she wanted to cook dinner, but Daniel found so many things in the kitchen made for frolic that she finally banned him.

"At this rate you'll never have anything to eat," she told him, and after nuzzling her neck he said, "You're the only thing I need. Low-calorie, too."

"Oh, you." She swatted him with the dish towel. "Out."

He pretended a pout till she kissed it away and told him the ban was only temporary. After he left she turned her attention to the caramel-glazed custard, New Orleans style. It was a recipe she'd found in one of Anne's cookbooks.

Skylar had never thought of herself as the domestic sort. She hadn't been the kind of little girl who tagged after her mother begging to make cookies. Over the years she'd done a fair amount of meal preparation for herself, but mostly she'd eaten in fast-food places or had take-out food right out of the box.

Her urge to cook surprised her as much as it did h
husband. Not that she planned to make a career of it. An
she certainly didn't plan to turn into a conventional wif
But she'd always prided herself on doing things well, an
the idea of preparing a gourmet meal for the husband sh
loved beyond imagining held great appeal for her.

She checked the trout amandine then began to prepa
the Caesar salad. Daniel stuck his head around the do
frame.

"It smells wonderful. May I come back in? I promise t
be good."

"You're always good, Daniel, and no, you can't com
in."

"What if I promise to behave?"

"Don't spread that boyish charm on me. If you want t
be helpful, go set the table."

"I already did that...it's lonely out here in the hall a
by myself."

"All right. I lift the ban." Laughing, he came in an
began to lift the lid on the soup pot. "Don't stick you
finger in. It's hot."

"Isn't it always?"

He grabbed her around the waist and kissed her until sh
forgot cooking. She forgot everything except him. The
kissed until the soup bubbled over, but by then neither o
them cared.

Daniel reached over and turned off the burner, the
turned his attention back to the matter of kissing.

"You're the best thing that ever happened to me, Sky,'
he said, and she knew he meant it.

She felt herself expanding inside and filling with ligh
Taking her husband by the hand she led him to the kitche
table and removed his clothes until he stood before he
naked and glorious, then she knelt and said, "Thank you

You're the best thing that ever happened to me, too.'' Said it without words. Said it with her entire being.

And finally Daniel lifted her up and spread her across the kitchen table and showed her how it was with them— desire that always shimmered beneath the surface, passion that took every opportunity to spill over its bounds until it finds release. Then afterward they gathered the remains of the soup, the half-finished salad and the cold trout aman- dine and carried them to the dining room where Daniel had set china plates and silver on linen napkins that glowed snowy white in the candlelight.

He pulled out her chair and sat at the head of the table, then lifted his wineglass and said, "To us. Daniel and Sky- lar Westmoreland, lovers forever."

"To us."

They drank their wine, a good Italian pinot grigio he'd brought up from the wine cellar. When they started on the salad he said, "You're too far away," then moved his place setting around the table and pulled up a chair so close to hers that they sat with their legs touching, naked skin still gleaming from their earlier exertions on the kitchen table.

They fed each other tidbits of salad, stopping often to kiss deeply and make soft murmurings of pleasure, and Skylar sighed.

"What is it, Sky?"

"I wish it could always be this way."

"It will. We'll keep our romance alive just as Mom and Dad have."

"Can we, Daniel? Even after we leave Belle Rose?"

"Of course."

Skylar wanted to believe him, and so she didn't remind him that Belle Rose was a beautiful cocoon, that high on their bluff overlooking two rivers they were cut off from

the rest of the world, protected from the opinions of other.
And the judgment.

Instead she lingered over dinner, savoring every deligh
ful, hedonistic moment, telling herself that she and Danie
could make time stand still. When the phone rang she wa
jarred back to the real world. Don't answer it, she wante
to say.

But of course Daniel did. How could he not? It could b
Anne calling with news of Michael. Or Hannah. Or Emily

"I'll be right back." He kissed her softly, then went int
the library and picked up the receiver. "Hello…"

Skylar tried not to listen. She even clanked silverwar
against china in an effort to shut out his words. "I'll driv
over tomorrow," she heard Daniel say, and although sh
didn't know what was being said at the other end of th
line, she knew it meant the end of their romantic idyll.

After he'd finished taking the call Daniel stood in th
doorway not saying a word, simply looking at her. Skyla
read his silence and she was afraid. Not for herself. But fo
them. For all the wonderful things they were together i
the protection of Daniel's ancestral home.

"Is it your dad?"

"No."

"Thank goodness," she said, but she was feeling no relief

He held her gaze for a long time before he finally sai
her name. "Skylar, we have to g—" She jumped out o
her chair and put her hand over his mouth.

"Shhh, don't say it, Daniel. Not yet."

He pulled her into his arms and held her for a very long
time. Over his shoulder and through the French doors she
could see that the moon was full and that it bathed the
garden in ethereal light. The garden looked unreal, fairy-
tale-like, a place of magic and enchantment, a place where
nothing bad could ever happen.

"When do you have to go, Daniel?"

"We. I'm taking you with me." He leaned back so he could see her face. "We'll leave in the morning."

"That gives us time," she said, then led him into the garden where the fragrance of ancient Bourbon roses perfumed the air and the stars seemed so close they were caught in Daniel's hair.

They stood underneath a magnolia tree holding on to each other as if all the forces of nature were trying to rip them apart. Then Skylar picked roses and scattered the petals on a lush bed of still-green grass and pulled Daniel down to her.

Blessed by moonlight and surrounded by the scent of roses, Skylar and Daniel loved each other, and when he suggested they go inside she said, "Can we stay here, Daniel?" for the place seemed sacred to her and she didn't want to break the spell.

He went inside and came back with quilts to ward off the evening chill and pillows to cushion their heads, and they slept in each other's arms until the dew came on the grass. Then they watched as the moon paled in the west and the sun sent its splendor across the eastern skies.

And their hearts were too full to speak.

Since it was early they decided to pick up breakfast and take it to the nursing home so they could eat with Anne while they told her the news. Daniel was glad for all the activity because it kept his mind off the business at hand: returning to Atlanta with a bride who would surely set his church on its ear.

He found his mother standing beside Michael's bed working with his feet and legs. "So he doesn't forget how to walk," she said when they went into the room.

Then she hugged them both very close. "Goodness, I didn't expect to see the two of you for days."

Daniel didn't want to break the news right away, possibly because as long as he didn't talk about it or think about it, it didn't seem quite real.

"I brought breakfast, Mom."

"Good. I woke up starving this morning." Anne tore the cover off a sausage and biscuit then passed it under Michael's nose. "Smell that, darling. Isn't that yummy? Why don't you wake up and have breakfast with me?"

Skylar reached for Daniel's hand, and he squeezed it gently, communicating without words their fear as well as their hope—fear that this could happen to them and the hope that they would have the kind of relationship Anne and Michael did. In love forever, no matter what their fate.

Daniel pulled three chairs close to the window and they ate together in the sunshine while he told his mother that he and Skylar were leaving.

"There was an unexpected death in my congregation."

"Anyone I know?"

"Brian Castles, chairman of my administrative board. It's not the best of times to take Skylar, but we don't have a choice."

"I think it'll be better this way," Skylar said. "I can blend in with the woodwork."

Daniel and Anne both laughed at the idea of Skylar blending in with anything. One of the things he loved most about his wife was her larger-than-life presence. He'd planned to call ahead and prepare his congregation for a new pastor's wife, give them a chance to plan some sort of reception for her. Skylar would shine at such an event, then, once they all got to know her...

Daniel stopped that line of thinking. No use borrowing trouble. Wasn't that what he always told everybody else? Faith and worry don't belong together.

"I hate to leave you in the lurch, Mom."

"Nonsense. Hannah's here. And besides that, I don't really need anyone with me all the time. Tranquility Manor is a second home for Michael and me. We feel sort of cozy here, kind of like being roommates at a boarding house."

Daniel saw through Anne's false cheer. There were lines on her face that had not been there before Michael vanished into his coma, and more gray hair than she'd ever had. Her easy grace was gone, and in its place was a forced optimism that dulled the familiar light in her eyes.

It would be so easy to fall back into the trap of shouting questions to the heavens. *Why? Why me?*

"You'll call me if you need me?" he asked.

"I will."

"Then Skylar and I will be going." He caught his mother's hand. "Let us pray," he said, and saying it felt natural and good. Joined in a circle of love he offered his thanks to a God who had never gone away.

"Thank you, Daniel. Will you do one more thing for me?"

"What's that?"

"Before you take my daughter-in-law away, I wonder if she'd sing for Michael."

Daniel glanced at his wife. "Sky?"

"Of course I will, Anne. Any song in particular?"

"Do you know 'Amazing Grace'?"

As Skylar began to sing, Daniel was not surprised that she knew the old hymn. The thing that knocked his socks off was the way she sang it…with such passion that he saw angels bending 'round his father's bed. A radiance filled the room, and when Skylar finished singing a hushed quiet fell upon them. Nobody spoke for fear of breaking the spell.

Daniel and Skylar kissed Anne then tiptoed toward the door. When he closed it behind him, he saw his mother lean down and kiss Michael and then reach for his diary.

Chapter Twenty-Eight

From the diary of Michael Westmoreland:

December 10, 1966

I got home from the Dolomites today and found out Anne is seeing someone else. What did I expect? She's the most remarkable woman I've ever met, and if I was fool enough to send her that stupid letter releasing her, then I deserve to live the rest of my life with the awful knowledge that I let the love of my life get away.

I think it was Hester Lynch Piozzi who said, "Character never changes; the acorn becomes an oak, which is very little like an acorn to be sure, but it never becomes an ash."

I should have remembered that before I told Anne that I wanted to spare her the trauma and worry of being the wife of a high-altitude filmmaker. Anne is no shrinking violet, no clinging vine (I'm full of clichés today. Maybe that's what heartbreak does to a man, sets him to thinking in tired circles.) She has courage and spunk and wit and warmth and charm and beauty....

I won't lose her. That's all. I can't, for to live my life without Anne at my side is to be half a man. I may as well go through my life missing an arm and a leg and the best part of my heart as to live without her.

I'll do whatever it takes to get her back. Including beg.

I have love on my side. True love. I hope that gives me an edge.

What was it Emily Dickinson said about hope...?

> Hope is the thing with feathers—
> That perches in the soul—
> And sings the tune without the words—
> And never stops—at all—

I have to believe that's true. I have to believe that I can win my beloved Anne once more, for to live without her is unthinkable.

Chapter Twenty-Nine

Don't cry, Anne. I'm trying to reach out to you. I'm trying to let you know I'm still here.

My arms are heavy, and my legs. Why won't they move? What is this deep paralysis that has overcome me? Thank God it hasn't overtaken my mind. Sometimes the fog closes in and I don't know things, don't quite hear, but not always.

For some reason I'm very clear today. I know that Daniel is married and I know that his wife has a voice that slices my heart. A rich, powerful, evocative voice that makes me want to rise up out of this bed and whisk Anne off to the Hawaiian Islands for six weeks of non-stop sex.

Why did I wait so long to take her there? Knowing how she'd always wanted to go? Did I think I was invincible? Did I believe that nothing bad could ever happen to me on that mountain?

I feel you, Anne. Come closer. That's right… Can you hear my thoughts? Remember how we used to try telepathy? It started as a game, sitting at the dining-room table after dinner, you trying to figure out which song title I was thinking of. You were very good at it. Remember?

Then later we decided we could use it while I was in the Himalayas and you were back home in Mississippi. I remember coming home that Christmas of '75 and asking you if you got the telepathic message I sent you. I remember how you blushed, and I knew without your saying a word that you had.

"Not in front of the children," you said. Later that night as we lay tangled together, worn out from making love as if we'd just returned to the home front and would both be leaving for war the next day, you said, "Michael, the next time you decide to have sex by telepathy, please wait until I'm home in bed."

"Why is that, my precious?" I said.

"I made a fool of myself in the grocery store. There I was with a cantaloupe in my hand moaning and trying to keep from carrying on."

Remember how we laughed till we had to hold on to each other to keep from falling off the bed? Then you said, "I did start a run on cantaloupes, though."

God, how I miss you, Anne.

Hang on. Just keep hanging on.

I'm coming back to you. I promise.

Chapter Thirty

Skylar was sitting in the back of the church trying to listen to the choir, but all she could think of was what the young man with the tight black pants had said when she'd entered the sanctuary.

"Wow, preacher! They said you'd married a woman named Skylar, but I never dreamed it would be *her*." Then he'd looked her up and down as if he could see right through her clothes and given a wolf whistle. Loud. So everybody turned around to stare. And right in front of Daniel.

Daniel had made light of it, of course. He'd said, "She is beautiful, isn't she, Jim?" But she could tell by the way he stiffened that he was anything except lighthearted as they'd walked on by with their heads held high.

"Where are we going?" she'd asked.

"To the front of the church. I want everybody to see that I've married the most wonderful woman in the world."

The way people were staring, she figured that nobody else shared his opinion, so she'd asked if he would please just seat her discreetly in the back instead of parading her around.

"Besides that makes more sense," she'd told him. "Then you can whisk off to your office and get into your robes."

He'd seated her beside an ancient woman with a hearing aid who'd smiled the whole time Daniel had introduced them and kept calling her Tyler while necks craned all over the church. She was used to that but with a far different crowd. The kind that frequented bars and nightclubs and concert halls. An appreciative crowd.

She was thankful when the service started and the gawkers turned their attention toward the front. The choir was singing some god-awful dirge-like number that could have used a lighter touch and a soloist who was in her comfortable range. If Skylar hadn't been so nervous about being on display she'd have been amused by the look on Daniel's face.

Laughter was close to the surface, and he was trying valiantly to keep it at bay. The struggle gave him the look of a little boy who knows he's being bad and is scared he's going to get caught. Fortunately the song came to an end, and the organist crash-banged her way into the offertory.

It was all very high church. Not at all the church of her upbringing, which was a great relief to Skylar. If Daniel's church had been one of those Bible-thumping, hell-fire-and-damnation kinds, she would never be able to come. *Never.*

And she wanted to. For Daniel's sake. She knew she would never be a model preacher's wife. She'd never be the kind who served side by side with her husband. But she *could* show her love and support of him by her attendance. She could and she *would* stand by his side as the parishioners filed out the church door.

Even if it killed her. And it just might. The way that old biddy across the aisle kept cutting her eyes back to Skylar told her everything she needed to know. Jim had already been talking.

Before the day was over, Skylar would be willing to bet that every member of Daniel's congregation would know that he'd married the star of *Too Hot to Handle*.

Skylar picked at her lunch and Daniel knew she was thinking about what Jim had said. Should he bring it up or let it lie? If he brought it up she would think the boy's rude remark carried a lot of weight with him, and he certainly didn't want that. On the other hand, if he didn't bring it out in the open it could fester and erupt at some later date.

"Skylar..."

She stood up so fast her chair toppled, then she launched herself into his lap. "Hold me, Daniel. Just hold me."

He picked her up and carried her upstairs to their bedroom. The sun was shining through the bank of west windows and he laid her tenderly on the bed in a circle of sunlight.

She pulled him down to her, fierce and hungry. They jerked at their clothing, tossing it in an untidy heap beside the bed, and came together with a passion that rocked Daniel to the depths of his very soul. He whispered her name against the soft fragrant skin of her neck and told her he loved her more than life itself, which probably would be considered a sacrilege to the likes of Lincoln Hodges who was chairman of the pastor/parish relations committee, but which made perfect sense to Daniel.

Somewhere he'd read that sex was the ultimate spiritual experience, and with Skylar that was so. Surrounded by her sweet hot flesh he knew the essence of the Universal Mind. *Love. All is love.*

He was in the midst of the most mind-shattering climax he'd ever had when the doorbell rang.

"Daniel?"

"Ignore it," he said through gritted teeth, then collapsed on her in a quivering heap. She stroked his back while the doorbell rang and rang.

"Darling, I don't think the caller is going away," she whispered.

"I believe you're right." He jumped into his clothes then ran his hand through his hair. "Do I look like a man who has been rudely interrupted while making love?"

"Yes."

"Good."

He leaned down and kissed his wife. Thoroughly. "Don't you move. I'll be right back."

He wasn't, though. Skylar scowled at the clock as if she could make it take back what it was saying. Daniel had been gone over an hour, and all her instincts told her that it was not good. His caller was probably an irate parishioner who wanted him to get a divorce immediately before they all decided to run him out of town on a rail for marrying her.

Not that she had ever considered her video anything except *art*. A bit on the wild side, but still within the bounds of decency. She remembered when she'd shot the video. Hal, the producer, had wanted her to ditch the shorts in favor of a G-string. She'd told him in no uncertain terms that she was a singer, not a stripper.

She and the band were supposed to do another video with Hal next spring, but she'd had reservations even as they'd discussed it last fall. And she certainly did now.

What was taking Daniel so long?

Skylar got out of bed, put on her robe and went into the kitchen to get a bite to eat. All of a sudden she was starving.

Daniel's visitor was none other than Lincoln Hodges, who sat with his hat on his knee as if he'd just come in for a quick hello instead of a lynching.

Daniel had expected this, but not so soon. He was less than prepared. In fact, he was vulnerable. Mellow from his rousing session in Skylar's arms.

"I don't know why nobody knew about this woman until today," Lincoln was saying.

"Her name is Skylar, and she's my wife."

"I meant no disrespect to you."

"None taken." Daniel couldn't help but notice the emphasis Lincoln put on the last word. Obviously he meant enormous disrespect toward Skylar.

"Still, you took us all by surprise and we never expected anything like…that."

"She is quite remarkable, isn't she? I fell in love with her the moment I saw her, and being a red-blooded male I didn't stop to ask anybody's permission."

Daniel hoped Lincoln would take the point without taking offense. He figured the best way to handle this situation was with a light hand. And from the looks of things it was already a *situation*.

"How come we didn't meet her at the funeral?"

"My job was to comfort the bereaved family. I didn't think it an appropriate time to introduce my wife."

"If we'd had even a little advance warning we could have been better prepared."

"Warning?"

Lincoln fiddled with his hat and got red in the face. "You know what I mean."

"I guess I don't, Lincoln. I'm married to a perfectly

lovely woman, and I expect you to extend her the same warm welcome you'd extend to any new member of this congregation."

"You married a porn star!"

Daniel was enraged and heartsick at the same time. This was worse than he expected. Far worse. He was glad the parsonage had been built with thick walls so that Skylar wouldn't hear.

It took every ounce of his willpower not to leap over the desk and throttle the man. Instead he gripped the arms of his chair so hard his knuckles turned white.

"Careful, Lincoln. That's my wife you're maligning."

"It's not me saying those things, Daniel. You know I support you a hundred percent."

"I'm glad to hear that. My wife will appreciate it as well."

"I'm just telling you things you ought to know. Everybody's talking."

"Gossip is a dangerous, hurtful thing. I trust you'll do everything in your power to squelch it."

"Lord God, preacher. How do you stop an avalanche? The ones who haven't seen that video have gone out to buy it."

Daniel made one last attempt at levity. "This will put her on the charts. Skylar will be pleased."

"You're not taking this seriously, Daniel."

"No, I'm taking it very seriously, Lincoln. But I'm also trusting that my congregation will have enough grace and charity to forgo judgment in favor of getting to know one of the most warm and loving women ever to come into their midst."

"Is that all you've got to say?"

"No. I'm trusting you to take a leadership role in making certain that my wife is welcomed into this church, Lincoln.

Warmly welcomed. Furthermore, I expect no breath of this sorry gossip will be repeated in her presence.''

"I'll do the best I can. It would help if you could tell me that she's made a complete change.''

"What do you mean?''

"She's giving up her career, isn't she?''

"No. I didn't ask her to and I don't expect her to.''

"Then I expect you'd better batten the hatches, Daniel, because you and that new wife of yours are in for a hell of a storm.''

After Lincoln had left, Daniel sat at his desk a long time trying to marshal his thoughts and regain his composure. He didn't mind a storm on his account. Every minister had to weather one from time to time. It was Skylar he worried about. Skylar he wanted to protect.

He found her in the kitchen eating an enormous peanut butter and jelly sandwich.

"Hi.'' Her smile didn't quite touch her eyes. "Want one, too?''

"That sounds good.''

She waited until her back was turned to ask, "What was that all about?''

He wished he could say, "Nothing,'' then take her back to bed and make love until his conversation with Lincoln was wiped from his mind. But the one thing he'd always admired about his parents' marriage was their honesty with each other. When he'd turned eighteen his father had taken him aside and said, "Son, some day you'll take a wife, and when you do there are two things I want you to remember: Tell her you love her every day, and always tell her the truth. Lies can ruin a marriage.''

Daniel slipped his arms around his wife from behind and said, "I love you, Skylar.''

She turned around with the peanut-butter knife in one

hand and a piece of bread in the other. "I know you do, Daniel, but you didn't answer my question."

"The answer is that the whole congregation has gone out to buy a copy of your video." She groaned and he kissed her long and hard. "Nothing's going to happen that we can't get through together. Do you hear me, Sky?"

"Yes. I hear you."

"Good." He kissed her again, then swept her into his arms. "I'm starving."

"You'll have to put me down. I can't reach the peanut-butter jar."

"Not for peanut butter." He carried her up the stairs and drew the curtains against the lengthening shadows, then spread his wife on the bed and made love to her until she fell asleep in his arms, sated and smiling.

Daniel pulled her so close he could feel her heart beating against his. "Hold on tight, Skylar," he whispered. "Hold on and don't let go. Don't ever let go."

Chapter Thirty-One

Monday came as a great relief to Skylar, and it struck her all of a sudden that this was how she'd felt growing up under the censure of her father and his congregation. She was standing in the middle of the parsonage's flower garden deadheading rose bushes and planning how she would get some good rose food to perk them up. Swamped by déjà vu she went as still as a doe caught in headlights, then dropped her basket and ran as fast as she could to find Daniel.

He was in the basement lifting weights, his body covered in a fine sheen of sweat, his T-shirt clinging to him in big damp patches. She ran straight to him. He dropped the weights and pulled her into his arms.

"Sky? What's wrong?"

"I have to talk to you."

"This sounds serious."

"It is. It's something I thought of in the garden and I can't wait another minute to clear it up."

"This sounds like a teacup conversation."

"What's that?"

He caught her hand and lead her upstairs, explaining all the while how his Grandmother Beaufort always told them that serious matters were best discussed over a good cup of English tea always served with honey, never sugar, and a generous dollop of real cream, not milk and *never* the artificial cream which she considered one of the scourges of modern society.

"Your grandmother must be a wise woman because I feel better already just talking about it."

"Sit." Daniel pulled out a chair for her, then said, "Start talking anytime you like," while he made the tea.

Skylar folded her hands in her lap and tried to compose herself. This would be one of the most important conversations she would ever have with her husband, and she wanted to get it right.

"Daniel, have I ever told you how much I enjoy what I do for a living?"

"No, but you didn't have to. It's obvious. No one could sing with such passion if they didn't love music and performing."

"In a way I suppose it's a calling as much as your ministry. Music is the universal language, and I can feel how my singing touches people. I can move them to tears or laughter, and I don't want to give that up."

"I didn't ask you to."

"I know, but I have a feeling your congregation will expect it of me."

Daniel set two cups of tea on the table, then reached for her hands. "No one has a right to tell you what to do. This is not even an issue, Skylar."

"It's easy to say that now, but what about when I'm on the road performing?"

The way he grinned made her fall in love with him all over again. "I think it's great being married to a celebrity. Do I get to come backstage and kiss the star?"

"You want to travel with me?"

"Not only want to, I'm planning to. Whenever I can."

Her husband's face was the dearest thing in the world to her, and she traced his fine cheekbones then his lips before she could speak.

"You keep surprising me."

"Good, Mrs. Westmoreland. I plan to do that the rest of our lives."

Skylar took a long sip of tea and felt how it did soothe the soul. "There's something else I have to tell you." He waited, watching her over the rim of his teacup. "What happened yesterday reminded me of all those years I endured as the object of censure right in the midst of Daddy's church. Mondays always felt like being released from prison. I don't want to feel that the rest of my life, Daniel."

"What are you saying, Sky?"

"I'm saying that I don't expect miracles here because people are only human. I want to be at your side, but if there are many repeat performances of yesterday, I know I won't bear them with grace."

He grinned again. "I would guess not. I know that stinger firsthand."

His generosity of spirit amazed Skylar, and what amazed her even more was her good fortune. How had she ever found a man like Daniel? What stroke of good fortune had set this absolute prince among men in her path?

Looking at his sweet smile and feeling his total adoration, she swore she would never do anything to bring harm to this man. She would walk over jagged glass before she would bring disaster to Daniel.

"All in all, I think it best if I don't even go to church. At least until all this blows over. Out of sight, out of mind. What do you think?"

"Skylar, I don't want you ever to think you have to put in an appearance for my sake or for the sake of anyone else. But I also don't want to think you're staying away from church or any other place you want to be because of anyone else. I like to think that people really do want to be good and loving and tolerant. Why don't we give them a little time, give them a chance to love you?"

Though she didn't share his view of other people's motives, she loved him enough to endure a while longer in order to put his theory to the test.

"I can do that."

"Good."

"Thank you for making this talk easy, Daniel."

"You're more than welcome." He pulled her into his arms and kissed her. "Always, my love."

He kissed her again, deeply this time, and she saw how her husband had the power to move her from loving gratitude to overwhelming desire in a matter of seconds. The thrill of his touch set off little bonfires underneath her skin, and she slid her hands under his shirt so she could touch his dampened skin.

"Hmmm. I want to lick that sweat off," she murmured, and he picked her up and carried her into the overgrown garden, telling her in the most erotic terms exactly what he intended to do to her.

"Here? In broad open daylight?"

"Yes." He grinned. "Thank God for tall brick walls."

Early the next morning while Skylar was in the shower singing "The Man I Love," Daniel called Hannah.

"I need you to rally the troops," he said.

"What's the problem, Daniel?"

He told her about the reaction of his congregation to Skylar. "When we walk into church Sunday I want Skylar to be flanked by family. I want everybody to see that she is not only approved by my family, she is beloved."

"Em and Jake will come. They're still in Atlanta. She said she was going to call you anyhow...some last-minute changes in their wedding plans."

"What?"

"She's being mysterious about everything. All she said was that it's top secret."

"What about you, Hannah. Can you come?"

"I can do even better than that. I'll send Mom."

"She won't leave Dad."

"I'll make her. If she doesn't take a break from being caregiver, I'm afraid we're going to have two sick people on our hands."

"She looks tired, but I don't think she's that bad."

"You don't know shit from Shinola, Daniel. You had your head in the clouds the whole time you were here."

"You could say that."

"I just did. I'll make reservations for Mom on the six o'clock flight. Friday."

"You'd better ask her first."

"Leave everything to me. All you have to do is be there at the airport to pick her up."

"Thanks, sis."

"Don't call me sis."

She hung up and Daniel sat at his desk laughing. "Lord help the poor man who falls in love with Hannah," he said, then he went upstairs and joined his wife in the shower.

It took them two hours to get clean.

Chapter Thirty-Two

From the diary of Anne Beaufort Westmoreland:

October 4, 2001

I'm leaving tomorrow for Atlanta. I still can't believe it. I don't know how I let Hannah talk me into it. Actually, I didn't. She used emotional blackmail. She said, "Dad would be mad as hell if he knew you let Daniel and Skylar down in order to hover over him. Besides, you know how he'd hate being treated like an invalid."

Oh, I know, I know. She's right. Michael is a strong man, full of pride. He must hate lying there flat on his back helpless, and apparently I'm not helping him one little bit, otherwise why isn't he awake?

And who knows? Maybe if I leave him for the weekend he'll get scared he's losing me and snap out of that coma just to make sure he doesn't.

Hannah will be here with Michael, of course. She has a new assignment, somewhere in Alaska I think, but she told her editor she couldn't leave for another couple of weeks. Until after her sister's wedding.

I heard her telling her dad all about it when I came in this afternoon. He was always so proud of his children. All of them. I still can't believe he's not going to wake up in time to give Emily away.

Of course, he didn't come back to us for Daniel's wedding, and I know he would never have missed that if he'd had a choice. Sometimes I think of this coma as an unknown power holding Michael hostage, a monster you'd shoot if you could see the whites of its eyes. If it's merely a medical phenomenon why can't the doctors bring him back?

Why can't I? The strongest force in the world is true love. I believe that. I always have. Then what am I doing wrong? What am I missing? I have to believe that Michael will return to me because of the power of his love, because he can't bear to live without me.

Because I can't bear to live without him...

Well...I'm crying again. I put my writing aside for a while and lay down beside Michael and told him I was leaving, then I kissed him long and hard, hoping for a response. Always hoping. Nada.

"Darling," I told him, "your children need you. Soon they'll all be married except Hannah. You're missing one of the most joyful times of your life."

Then I showed him the pictures we took of Daniel's wedding. I put them in his hand so he could feel the slick surface, then I held them in front of his face hoping he'd sense them there and open his eyes. "Look, Michael," I said, "please open your eyes and look."

I searched and searched for some sign that he was

trying to come back, and when I didn't see anything I got so mad at him I had to go into the bathroom and hold a washcloth over my mouth so he wouldn't hear me scream.

Now I'm ashamed of myself. I'm going to sit on the side of his bed and put the pictures in his hand and describe them one by one. I'm not going to leave out a single detail. I want Daniel's wedding to be so real to Michael that he feels as if he didn't miss a thing.

Then I'm going to take off my clothes and lie beside him all night long hugging him. I'm not going to sleep a wink. I want to keep a vigil. In case I've been missing something in the dark.

Chapter Thirty-Three

I feel you lying beside me, Anne. I feel how tense you are. I wish I could soothe you. I'm trying so hard to get my hands to move. I want to massage your neck. You always collect tension at the back of your neck.

It's October, you told me. Unbelievable. More than four months of my life vanished without a trace.

That's not exactly true. So much has happened while I've been sleeping. I have a daughter-in-law I've never seen, and soon I'll have a son-in-law.

The deep fog is lifting, Annie. I wish I could tell you that. I wish I had some way of letting you know. My mind is clearer now, not wrapped in cotton batting. I still can't keep up with the days and weeks and months slipping by, but I'm vaguely aware of the passage of time.

I know it's morning by the sounds coming from the hallway. Breakfast trays rattling. Rubber-wheeled carts squeaking. I know nighttime because you're always here. When the sun shines I know midmorning because of the warmth on my face. Halfway between the breakfast trays and the lunch trays.

I wish I could say all this to you. I don't want you to lose hope. I don't want you to give up on me.

But you won't. I know that. You're made of stronger stuff. You have more courage than anyone I know, including seasoned climbers who have tackled the world's most intimidating peaks.

Besides that, we are bound forever by true love. And true love is worth any price, you once told me. I agree. And yet I never had to pay a price. You did. You could have been famous. You were that good. Still could be with some practice. I hope you're not neglecting your music while I'm here, Anne. I hope you're not letting the baby grand collect dust.

I used to wonder if you ever regretted giving up your career. Lately I've been thinking about that, about how you sacrificed everything for me, and now you're left behind with nothing but a shell. Of course you have the children, but they're grown. Lord, I remember what a handful they were when they were young. You used to say they spent the first two years of their lives trying to commit suicide, and the next six trying to commit murder. Remember that time Hannah climbed into Daniel's bed while he was napping and you found her holding a teddy bear over his face? All she'd wanted to do, she said, was have a teddy bear picnic with her little brother like the story you'd read. She was three, he was two.

I was in Alaska when that happened. When I returned to Belle Rose I found you sitting in the laundry room on top of the washing machine sipping your tea like a queen. You said, "It's the only place safe from our hellions, Michael. You know they hate the washer and dryer." Then you gave me that beautiful smile I fell in love with the day I met you and said, ''Besides, I like the vibration, reminds me of you.''

I took your teacup out of your hand and said, ''Let me give you the real thing.''

And I did. Right there on top of the washing machine. I think that was when you got pregnant with Emily.

God, how I loved you then. How I love you now.

Chapter Thirty-Four

Standing beside the old rosewood upright piano in the parsonage singing while Daniel's mother played a jazzy version of "Come Rain or Come Shine," Skylar knew the meaning of family for the first time in her life. Daniel was sitting on the sofa beside Emily beaming as if he'd invented music, and Jake flanked her on the other side. They were sitting close together holding hands and occasionally bending toward each other for a kiss.

Out of the blue a panicked feeling came over Skylar as if this were her one last chance at a happy life and somehow she was blowing it. She faltered on the words, and Daniel's mother looked up from the keyboard at her.

Skylar cleared her throat and said, "Frog...will you excuse me a moment?" Then she hurried to the kitchen and poured herself a glass of water. She was leaning against the sink drinking the whole thing in one big gulp when Daniel came in.

He put his arms around her and said, "Everything all right?"

"Yes." She smiled at him but her face felt tight and unnatural. Then she looked at her husband and knew he knew she'd just lied and so she said, "I don't know what happened, Daniel. All of sudden I got scared."

"I shouldn't have asked my family here tonight. It's too much for you, too soon."

"No, no. It's not that. I love having them here. Really, I do, Daniel. Your mother is wonderful, and Emily and Jake are lots of fun."

Daniel was rubbing her back and looking at her with such a look of love that she felt foolish. What was the matter with her?

"You're sure?"

"Positive." With Daniel nearby touching her she felt safe. More than safe, really. She felt practically invincible. Somehow she'd stumbled into a remarkable new life where nobody was ever going to tell her she was wasn't worth a hill of beans. "You go back in there with your family and I'll fix some lemonade. How does that sound?"

"Perfect." He kissed her, long and hard. She wanted to grab hold of him and not let go just in case.... In case she'd wake up tomorrow and find out she'd dreamed the whole thing and she was smack-dab back in the middle of her earlier life. "You're perfect," he added, and she ran her hands inside his shirt and made little humming sounds of satisfaction because she was too full to speak and that was the only way she knew to say, "You're perfect, too."

Later that night after Emily and Jake had gone back to his apartment and Anne was asleep in the guest room, Skylar made love with her husband until she was both reenergized and exhausted. Then she lay in his arms listening to the even sounds of his breathing as he slept, lay with her eyes wide open so she could see what was coming around the corner.

Daniel's ploy had worked. That's what he was thinking while the choir sang "Swing Low, Sweet Chariot." It was a rousing number that should have held his complete attention. Instead he was focused on his wife sitting in the front pew flanked by his mother and his sister. She was wearing blue and she looked beautiful. More than that, she looked happy.

Anne Beaufort Westmoreland was beloved by Daniel's congregation, and when she'd walked in with her daughter-in-law the whole atmosphere changed. People who had stood at a distance and judged the previous Sunday had come over to meet Skylar. If their friendliness was a little guarded, that was okay. All they needed was time. Time, plus a good nudge from their pastor.

With the last notes of the song fading, Daniel strode to the pulpit.

Chapter Thirty-Five

From the diary of Anne Beaufort Westmoreland:

October 8, 2001

How Michael would have loved Daniel's sermon. I wouldn't have missed it for the world. Hannah nearly died laughing when I told her about it.

"He gave 'em hell," she said, and I said, "Yes, but in a loving and gentle way."

Oh, I wish Michael could have been there to hear it. Naturally I knew what it was all about. The minute Daniel started talking about tolerance I knew he was slapping their hands for judging his wife. I ordered a tape, which should be here in the middle of the week so Michael can hear it. Basically, though, my son talked about how we should all be the kind of people who are known for our kindness and tolerance, for the things we love and accept rather than the things we criticize and ostracize. Oh, it was beautiful, *beautiful*.

Clarice wants a tape, too. She adores Daniel. I didn't know until last night the part she'd played in his match with Skylar. She came over for dinner. Usually I'm at the nursing home by then, but both Hannah and Clarice insisted.

"You've got to start living your life again, Anne," Clarice told me, and I said, "I thought that's what I've been doing," but she shot me right out of the saddle. I started to tell her, "You mind your little red wagon and I'll mind mine." But she's been too good to me. I couldn't say such a smart-mouthed thing and face myself in the mirror.

Of course, she's right about starting to live again. I feel as if I'm stuck in an airplane in a holding pattern.

Well, I guess all that's fixing to change. And very soon. You could have knocked me over with a feather when Emily and Jake sprang their surprise on us. Daniel didn't blink an eye, of course. He's so steady. Fortunately Hannah is all for the idea, otherwise she'd have had plenty to say.

Clarice approves, too. She volunteered to stay with Michael, and I said to her, "Don't you dare flirt with my husband while I'm gone," and she twitched her nose at me just like Elizabeth Montgomery on that old TV show "Bewitched" and said, "Well I just might."

She was kidding of course. We both were. And it felt good.

That brief outing to Atlanta was good for me. Made me feel almost like my old self. Lord, I'm getting older every day. I hate the way my upper arms are starting to sag. (Clarice said she'd buy me some six-pound weights, that they worked wonders. I guess they do. She's always strutting around in strapless tops.) I told Michael this morning that if he didn't return to me soon he wouldn't even recognize me.

Now that the wedding plans have changed I'll have to get a different outfit. Silk dresses and high heels are out.

I haven't told Michael about the change in plans. Emily and Jake are coming tomorrow to tell him. They didn't say so, but I think they're both counting on this drastic measure to bring Michael out of his coma.

I hope so. Oh, I really hope so.

Chapter Thirty-Six

Skylar was so proud of her husband that she wanted to stand on the rooftops and shout her pride to the world. Instead she decided to surprise him with a little exotic lingerie from Victoria's Secret. He'd wanted to come with her to the mall, saying she didn't know Atlanta that well yet. She'd had to say, "Daniel, I've been finding my way around since I was sixteen," and then because he'd looked both chagrined and disappointed she added, "Why don't you meet me for dinner?"

She was standing in front of Ruby Tuesday's holding a bag with her fancy new black lace nightgown when somebody recognized her. A teenager still in braces.

"Hey, it's Skylar Tate," he called, and suddenly she was surrounded by young people seeking autographs. It wasn't the sort of mob Elvis would attract, still it was gratifying. All her years of hard work were finally paying off.

The only downside of this impromptu autograph session

was that she had absolutely no protection, no band behind her back, no security guard to control the crowd if they became rowdy.

"Do you mind signing this?" Somebody thrust his tennis shoe at her, and she began to glance over their heads for Daniel. Not that she needed help. She'd been taking care of herself for as long as she could remember. Still, the crowd was mostly male. She'd forgotten how large teen-aged boys could be, man-sized and full of hormones.

She signed the tennis shoe then decided to call it quits before things got out of hand. Who knew what they would thrust her way next? Besides, it was beginning to get dark.

"That's all for today. Thanks for buying my albums." She recapped her pen and put it in her purse. The crowd began to drift away.

"It's not the music we love. It's the bod."

Skylar flinched. The voice had come from a strapping young man with a green Mohawk. She scanned the parking lot. Where was Daniel?

She decided to ignore the remark, and turned to go into the restaurant. Suddenly she found herself backed against the wall by three behemoths. Twice her weight and nearly a foot taller.

"Where you goin'?" This was from the one with the Mohawk, apparently the leader. The others leered at her.

"I'm meeting my husband."

"He won't mind waiting. Not for something as hot as you." They pressed closer. "Come on, Foxy, show us your stuff."

Skylar tried to see around them. Where was everybody? Didn't people eat on Mondays? Why didn't somebody passing through the parking lot see what was going on?

It wouldn't do to show fear. The meek don't inherit the earth: they get mugged. That's what Skylar had learned the hard way when she was eighteen and backpacking through the Smokies.

"Back off," she yelled.

They laughed. "You a reg'lar little wildcat, ain't you?" They began to circle her, meowing.

This was getting serious. And dangerous. Physically she was no match for them. Her only alternative was to scream.

She opened her mouth, and Mohawk clamped a big hand over it. He ripped her blouse while another grabbed her bag and held up the sexy nightie.

"Woowee, looka what we got here."

"Gimme that, Snake." Mohawk snagged the gown with one hand and kept her pinned to the wall with the other. "Let's see her in this."

"Not here, you fool. Cop's liable to come along." They were going to kidnap her and do things she couldn't bear to think about. But not without a fight.

She started kicking for all she was worth. Judging by the yowl of pain, she'd put one foot right where it hurt the most.

"Grab her legs, Jute!"

"I wouldn't do that if I were you." Skylar was released so fast she slid down the wall into a heap. All she saw was the blue uniform before she fainted.

Daniel hadn't stopped shaking inside since he'd found Skylar lying in a heap at the mall. She wouldn't let him call a doctor. She wouldn't even take a sedative. She'd said she was all right. He'd held her all night long, soothing her as if she were a baby. Sometime early this morning she'd finally fallen into an exhausted sleep.

He hadn't left her side except to get the paper and a cup of coffee. Sitting beside the window Daniel kept watch over his wife. He hadn't let himself think about what might have happened if the mall's security guard hadn't come along. All three young men had been arrested. Skylar hadn't backed down about pressing assault charges.

A city that spawned that kind of violence wasn't a place Daniel wanted to live. He'd worked hard to get where he was, one of the youngest ministers ever to be appointed to such a large church. There was talk that within the next five years he'd probably be appointed District Superintendent of the North Georgia Methodist Conference. Some insiders said he was being groomed for bishop.

Daniel had thought that was what he wanted...until now. His wife twisted restlessly on the bed, and he walked over to smooth the covers and caress her face. Such a dear face. He would die if he lost her.

She twisted away from him. "No no no..."

"Sky..." He cradled her in his arms and pressed her head against his chest. "Darling, it's all right. I'm here."

"Daniel..." She pushed back and smiled at him, but he wasn't fooled. It didn't touch her eyes. "Shouldn't you be at your office?"

"No. This is where I should be."

"But what about your job?"

"Don't worry. My secretary will call me if something comes up." He rocked her in slow tender motion until he could feel her relax. "Are you hungry? I've made sandwiches."

"You did?" This time her smile was genuine. "That sounds delicious." She started to swing her feet over the bed and he pressed her back to the covers. "Stay right here, young lady. You're getting breakfast in bed."

"That sounds wonderful, but I'm not an invalid, you know."

He leaned down to cup her face and kiss her. "Let me

take care of you, Sky.'' She nodded, and he could see how close she was to tears. "I'll be right back.''

He heated her sandwich, then added plenty of chips and a glass of orange juice and started toward the stairs. At the last minute he detoured by the garden and plucked a spectacular pink rose.

Skylar was sitting in bed reading the morning paper, her face blanched, her eyes brimming with unshed tears. Daniel could have kicked himself.

"Why didn't you tell me?'' she asked.

He took the paper from her and folded it so the damning article was hidden, then took both her hands. "Sky, listen to me. It doesn't matter.''

"The press said awful things.'' She jerked the paper back and pointed to the headlines. Skylar Tate Proves Too Hot To Handle, they screamed. And underneath, The Preacher And The Video Queen. The story was not journalism: it was pure sensationalism. An enterprising reporter had mined Skylar's past for nuggets that could be twisted to fit his sick slant on her career as well as her marriage to Daniel.

"The people who know us are not going to believe any of it, Sky. It'll all blow over in a few days. Nothing dies down quicker than yesterday's news.''

Daniel hoped that what he was saying was true. But he could tell his wife didn't believe him. He sat on the bed and put his arms around her.

Skylar felt as if she were put together with steel rods. She'd known from the beginning of her career that she would sometimes be a target for the tabloid sheets, but she hadn't thought they'd go after Daniel, too. Fortunately they hadn't put anything in about his drinking bout at Babe's, but they had uncovered the fact that he'd had his wedding reception there.

How could she have been so foolish? Why hadn't she thought of the consequences? She'd been so determined to remain independent that she'd let her own needs cloud her judgment.

"Everything will be all right, Sky."

Despair was in his face. She was being selfish again. Skylar cupped her husband's face and kissed him. "Of course it will," she whispered, then pulled him down to her and made a tent of the sheets. "Welcome to my harem."

There. She'd made him laugh. Taking little nibbles and lots of time she worked her way down from his neck to his groin. It was only when they were joined that she understood she'd needed this as much as he. Probably more.

With Daniel she erased the ugly details of yesterday and replaced them with what would later become sweet memories of today. The sandwich lay forgotten on the tray, and the sun tracked its way across the sky.

And when they finally lay in each other's arms sated and content, Skylar whispered, "Even if I never have another moment with you, I am blessed."

"Don't say that, Sky. We have the rest of our lives together." He traced the small bones of her arm, marveling aloud at how delicate she seemed, and she was repeating that old chestnut about looks being deceiving when the phone rang.

Daniel picked up the phone. Skylar was too languid and satisfied to pay much attention until he said, "Who called this emergency meeting?"

Skylar shivered as if a winter storm had invaded their bedroom. Every instinct she had was crying, Danger.

"What was that all about?" She could tell Daniel didn't want to tell her, but knew he would anyway. He was too honest to do otherwise.

"Lincoln Hodges and a few others want to talk to me."

She could guess the topic, so she didn't ask. "When?"

"Tomorrow morning. Nine."

Her heart sank. They would crucify him. And all because of her. "I suppose you have lots of preparation to do."

"No. I thought I'd mulch the roses before I do hospital visitation. Do you want to help?"

"With the roses or the visitation?"

Suddenly he smiled. "Why didn't I think of that? The hospital…what a great idea. You can sing to the patients…if you will."

"Do you think they'll want me to?"

"At least some of them. We'll ask first…you're sure you don't mind?"

How could she mind? She'd do anything to rectify the situation she'd created. It was not only embarrassing for Daniel, it was probably going to cost him his job. Singing a few songs at the hospital was probably tantamount to spitting on a forest fire, but she would do it to make Daniel feel better if nothing else.

Dreams disturbed Daniel. He reached for Skylar and came up with a handful of pillow. Groping in the semi-darkness of early dawn he said, "Sky…Skylar…"

She wasn't there. He sat up with his heart pounding and snapped on the light. She was probably in the bathroom. That was it. He'd go tearing in there and find her and feel ridiculous. And maybe scare her, besides.

He would wait. Stacking her pillow under his, he propped himself up and waited five seconds before alarm bells clanged in his head. There was no light coming from the bathroom. Not even a small slit.

Daniel bolted out of bed. "Skylar!" He flung open the bathroom door and it was empty. Without a stitch he raced down the stairs calling her name. He tripped over a wrinkle in the area rug at the foot of the stairs and nearly toppled. He was going to break his neck if he didn't slow down.

She was probably in the kitchen making coffee. Or eating a snack. Didn't he get hungry in the middle of the night? Especially after such a strenuous night.

Daniel made himself calm down, forced himself to snap on lights, told himself he was being an alarmist. The sun was beginning to pink the sky when he went into the kitchen and turned on the light. The first thing he saw was the note. Lying on the table underneath the salt shaker. Purple paper. Skylar's signature color.

Daniel sat down and stared at her handwriting. He didn't have to open it to know the contents. *Please, please, please,* he prayed, then pulled the folded sheet out of the envelope that simply said Daniel, in Skylar's dramatic script. Her ring fell out with the paper.

Tears started streaming even before he began to read.

My Darling,
By the time you read this I will be gone. Please don't try to find me. I've already done enough damage to you and your family. I can't stand by and watch them (the pastor/parish committee) destroy you.

Tell them I've gone and I won't be back. They won't have to worry anymore about me bringing shame to your ministry. I hope that fixes things for you. I hope it's not too late.

I love you, my precious Daniel. I will love you forever.

Skylar

Chapter Thirty-Seven

She'd thrown a few clothes and her cat into her car and left Atlanta before dawn. Birmingham was coming up, but Skylar was crying so hard she could barely see the signs. Her cat rubbed against her thigh and meowed.

"Hush up, Pussy Willow. It's the right thing to do."

The sign said Slow To 50. She was in the generic strip that metropolitan areas have—fast-food chains and video stores. The golden arches blurred, and so did Kentucky Fried Chicken. She was hungry but she didn't want to stop. If she did she would think of how she'd left Daniel sleeping with a half smile on his face, and then she wouldn't have the willpower to go on.

"Stop looking at me like that, P.W. This is the only way to do it."

The gas gauge fell into the red zone and she began to search for a place to stop. Just up ahead she saw a sign for gas. She didn't even bother to wipe her face. Who cared how she looked?

The main question was this: Where was she going? Her only thought had been to get away, her motive, to save Daniel.

After she'd paid for her gas, she got back into the car and just drove. West. Toward nowhere.

Daniel kept making up rules for himself: If Skylar's not back when I return from the meeting, I'll call somebody. When that deadline passed he decided it would be disloyal to Skylar to call anyone, even family. Just in case she'd merely needed some time to think and was already on her way back home.

Next he said to himself, If she's not back by dinnertime I'm calling Hannah. At six he stared at the clock and ate tuna straight out of the can while pacing the floor, all the while telling himself, She'll be back before dark.

By eleven o'clock he knew she wasn't coming back, and so he picked up the phone and called Hannah. "Be there," he said as he dialed the number of Belle Rose.

His sister picked up on the second ring. "Daniel...what are you doing calling this time of night?"

Daniel's throat clogged up and his chest felt tight. He could tell Hannah anything and she would understand. He had to keep telling himself that.

"Skylar's gone."

"Gone where?"

"I don't know."

Hannah digested this information silently, and when she spoke she sounded calm and authoritative, which was exactly what Daniel had counted on.

"What happened?" she asked, and Daniel told her, not leaving out a single detail.

And even though Skylar's note was intensely personal, he knew he could share it with Hannah because she loved both of them and would guard their secrets with her life if necessary. Hannah was that true-blue. Somebody you could always count on. The soldier you wanted beside you in the trenches when bombs were exploding around you and hand grenades were being lobbed your way.

After she'd heard the note, Hannah said, "I'm so sorry, Daniel. Of course you will search for her. All of us will."

"I don't want Mom to know. Not unless it becomes absolutely necessary."

"That goes without saying, Daniel."

"Nor Emily and Jake. It's too close to their wedding, and I don't want to spoil things for them."

"I agree. Do you have any idea where she might have gone?"

"Why don't you check her house in Vicksburg in the morning?"

"I'll do it tonight. I'll check Babe's, too. She seems to be close with the owner. What about the members of her band?"

"I don't know anything about them." It hit Daniel how awful that was, not to know the names of his wife's friends, where they lived, how they looked, nothing at all. Right then and there he vowed that as soon as Skylar came back they were going to take a real honeymoon, a trip somewhere far away from Vicksburg and Belle Rose and Tranquility Manor and Atlanta, somewhere removed from problems so they could really get to know each other. "That's the awful thing, Hannah. I simply don't have a clue who my wife would turn to in times of trouble."

"We'll get through this, Daniel. Together."

After they'd hung up he went outside to the garden and looked up at the night sky. Maybe it was the peace of gardens in general or perhaps it was the awesome beauty of the stars, but being outdoors always made Daniel feel closer to God. He tried to pray. He tried to form a powerful petition that would cover all the bases, but all he could do was groan out his agony.

And perhaps that was the most powerful prayer of all.

Skylar didn't stop until she was so hungry she thought she would faint. She didn't even know where she was. She'd stopped looking at signs three hours ago.

As soon as she'd stopped, Pussy Willow jumped out of the car with her and they both stretched their legs. "Where are we, P.W.?" The cat meowed once, and Skylar pushed her sunglasses down and searched for something that would give her a clue. The bank across the street did.

She was in Winfield, Alabama. It seemed as good a place as any to spend the night.

She checked into a motel without asking if they took pets. She was too exhausted to drive on if they said no. After she'd stowed her cat and her bag, she went in search of a drugstore and bought the strongest over-the-counter sleeping pill they had. Next she got two Quarter Pounders, one for herself and one for her cat.

They ate sitting side by side on the floor, then Skylar took two pills, pulled off her shoes and stretched out on top of the bed with her clothes still on. She didn't care about comfort. All she wanted was oblivion.

Daniel grabbed the phone before it had completed the first ring. "Hannah? Did you find her?"

"No. She's not at her house unless she's parked her car somewhere else, at a friend's or somewhere and is holed up inside. It wasn't at Babe's either. I'm so sorry, Daniel."

"What about Pete?"

"I'll call him first thing tomorrow morning. I don't know

how loyal he is to her, whether he'd lie for her, but if he tries to stonewall I can certainly find out where he lives.''

''Hannah, I don't know what I'd do without you.''

For once she didn't dish out a retort such as, You'd probably make a mess of things without me. Instead she said, ''We still have lots of options. Clarice, for one. Didn't you tell me she knew Skylar when she was growing up in Huntsville?''

''It must have been Clarice. I hate to bring her in on this. I don't want to worry her.''

''She'd want to help. Anyway, the main thing is to find Skylar.''

''Hannah?''

''What will I do when I find her?''

The long silence told Daniel more about his sister than anything. She was not the kind of person who flung opinions just to hear the sound of her own voice; she was the kind who pondered the problem then came up with a sensible solution.

''I don't know the answer to that, Daniel. She's a strong-willed woman. Apparently she's made up her mind, and she won't be easily swayed.''

''How well I know.'' Daniel was surprised that he could laugh. ''That's one of the things I love about her.''

''I guess you'll just have to follow your instincts.''

''I'll follow my heart.''

''Isn't that the same thing?''

''When all this is over, we'll have that philosophical debate.''

''Is that a promise?''

''It's a promise.''

Skylar woke up in the dark, and for a moment she didn't know where she was. She was wearing all her clothes and couldn't remember why.

"Daniel?"

She reached across the bed for her husband. Outside somebody slammed a car door, then let out a string of curses.

Then Skylar remembered, and the blues wrenched her so hard she curled into the fetal position and moaned. Pussy Willow jumped onto the bed and walked along the ridges of her body with dainty cat steps. Then she curved herself into Skylar's neck and meowed in her ear.

"Not now, P.W." She didn't care if she never moved again. She didn't care if her cat wet all over her. She didn't care about anything anymore.

Not even music.

Skylar didn't know how long she lay there, or whether she slept. All she knew was that a thin line of pink painted the mustard-colored bedspread and her bones felt welded together. If she didn't move somebody would have to take a crowbar and pry her legs apart from her torso.

She eased out of bed. P.W. was sitting at the door with her back to Skylar. Offended. Queen of the hill only nobody was paying attention.

Without even grabbing her shoes, Skylar opened the door and carried her cat around to the back of the small motel where they found a patch of dew-wet grass. P.W. minced around in a finicky way that usually made Skylar laugh.

Not today. Her laugh box was broken. Nothing could fix it except Daniel, and he was gone forever.

At the thought of her husband, Skylar felt as if somebody had taken a sledgehammer to her heart. "I did the right thing," she whispered, and P.W. gave her such a look of disdain, she cringed.

Hadn't she? All of a sudden she heard her daddy's voice:

Lie down with dogs, get up with fleas. She had infested Daniel. She'd infested his whole family, but now that she was gone they could make repairs. They could get on with their lives, and pretty soon if somebody mentioned Skylar Tate they would hardly remember her name.

Liar.

She sank onto the cracked concrete sidewalk and propped her chin on her hands. That's how heavy her head was. It needed support to stay erect. Her heart too. Except how was she ever going to prop it up?

With music.

While P.W. had been doing her business and Skylar had been moping, the sun had continued to rise and now she felt the heat of it on her right arm. That meant she was facing north toward Huntsville. North toward home.

All the years she'd spent in Alabama propping herself up with music washed over Skylar, and she knew what she had to do. Finally she knew where she was headed.

She stood up and dusted off the seat of her pants. Not full of life, but suddenly full of purpose. And for now that would keep her going. She'd wouldn't think about tomorrow at all. If the South's best-known fictional belle could do it, so could she.

"Let's go, P.W. It's time to be moving on."

Chapter Thirty-Eight

From the diary of Anne Beaufort Westmoreland:

October 9, 2001

I haven't seen Hannah all day. She called this morning to say she had something important to take care of. She didn't say what, but that's not unusual. Hannah is not known for telling her business.

Emily's a different story. Usually. Though I'll have to admit that this business with the change in wedding plans took us all by surprise. She called a little while ago and said she and Jake will be here late tonight. That they'd probably crash at Belle Rose so Michael would be fresh when they told him about the wedding plans.

I wish I thought the same thing: that Michael would be fresh in the morning, filled with some sort of new-found energy and rarin' to go (or some such old saying).

I'm afraid that Em's living in a dream world. I know, I know. I was the same way. Right before Michael and I got married you could have smashed me upside the head with a two-by-four and I wouldn't even have known I'd been hit. I was that lost in my own world, that deep in the fog of love.

Still am. Deep in the fog of love. After all these years.

Folks used to come up to us at parties and say, "Anne, I've never seen any two people who loved each other as deeply as you and Michael." Then they would ask, "How do you do it?"

I never knew what to tell them. If they had asked Michael he would have had a ready answer. And a brilliant one. That's why I nicknamed him the Brain. His enormous intelligence was apparent from the moment I met him. I used to tell him I fell in love with his brain first, and I guess that's true, though I try not to decipher love. Picking a thing apart destroys the magic.

There. That's the answer. That's what I should have told all those people through the years who wondered how Michael and I kept our love so fresh, that it appeared we'd just that moment fallen for each other.

Magic. That's the key.

Chapter Thirty-Nine

You couldn't miss the Saturn 5 rocket. It rose up out of the skyline, majestic and phallic, dwarfing everything around it. The minute she saw it Skylar had to take the next exit and pull her car into the first parking lot she came to in order to lean her head against the steering wheel and compose herself. That was the effect Huntsville always had on her. So many memories. And every one of them visceral.

Pussy Willow leaped onto her shoulder and peered into her face. When Skylar ignored her, the cat slunk to the back seat of the car and sat there in high dudgeon, a queen without an audience.

A tapping on her window startled Skylar, and she looked up to see a gray-haired man wearing a blue shirt with Carl embroidered on the pocket in red.

"Is anything wrong, ma'am?"

Even though she felt rotten, the courteous form of address made Skylar smile. That was one of the things she loved about the South. Men Carl's age and older had had mommas who made sure their children learned manners, whether they wanted to or not.

"I'm fine." She was lying, of course. The man she loved was in another city, another state. As long as they were apart she would never be *fine*. "Thanks for asking."

"Need any gas?"

"No, I was just resting a minute. I've come a long way."

Carl gave her fender a little pat and said, "Take care of yourself now, you hear?"

She was trying. Oh, she was trying.

As she drove out of the parking lot and back onto 565 memories swamped Skylar once more, threatening to drown her. She anchored herself to the steering wheel, tilted her chin high and kept on driving. She had places to go, things to do. Until she came face-to-face with her history and said, "You don't scare me anymore, you don't control me," she would never be free. She would always have to keep on running.

She left 565 and headed north toward the Tennessee line, north toward a little community in the foothills where country folk could walk to church every Sunday and listen to a man they called Preacher Tate exhort them to go home and sin no more.

Skylar didn't stop until she'd come to a white frame church tucked into what had once been a cow pasture. The door was open.

She walked in and sat down on the back pew and waited. Instead of hearing her father's voice as she'd expected, she heard music. The old hymns. "Bringing in the Sheaves." "Shall We Gather at the River." "Love Lifted Me."

At first Skylar hummed softly to the melody, and then she opened her mouth and began to sing.

* * *

His first night without his wife was agony. The second, hell. Daniel thought he would probably have gone crazy if Hannah hadn't called the next day with news of Skylar.

"Pete knows where she is, Daniel."

"Where?"

"He wouldn't say. He wants to talk to you first."

Driving was too slow, so Daniel flew. Hannah met him at the airport.

"You look like hell, Daniel. Have you slept?"

"Not much."

"Pete's waiting for us." They hurried to the car she'd rented while she was home. "When was the last time you shaved?"

"I don't remember."

"Everything's going to be all right, Daniel."

"You haven't said anything to Mom?"

"No. There's no need. Skylar will be back before Em's wedding, and Mom will never know."

They were silent the rest of the way to Pete's house. He met them at the door then ushered them into a den filled with framed photographs, most of them featuring Skylar.

"From the early days of the band," Pete said as Daniel walked from photograph to photograph looking. And aching.

There was Skylar in jeans and a T-shirt, her hair pulled back in a ponytail, standing in front of the microphone with the band behind her. She looked about eighteen. There she was in front of the Tower of London, Pete on the left and the other members of the band on the right. And there… Skylar alone, a faraway look in her eyes, gazing into the distance.

When Daniel sat down he was so full he couldn't speak. Hannah knew, and saved him.

"Pete said there were a few things he had to find out from you before he's willing to reveal her whereabouts."

Daniel nodded, and Pete began to talk. "I know the two of you had a whirlwind courtship. How much do you know about Skylar?"

Daniel not only told him what he knew of her background, but also told him the gist of her note, which gave her motive for leaving.

"That's Skylar. She's been running all her life. What do you plan to say to her when you see her?"

"I don't know. I probably should be thinking up arguments strong enough to compel her to come back to me, but I won't do that to her. I won't make her feel guilty or use words such as *commitment*. Marriage is not an institution, as some believe. It's an affair of the heart."

"Damn right," Pete said. Hannah didn't venture an opinion, which meant she thought she was out of her depth on this particular subject.

"I guess I'll tell her I love her and want her, no matter what, then leave the rest up to her. Make no mistake about it. I want Skylar. But I want her to come to me of her own free will."

"Good." Pete smiled.

"Does that mean I've passed the test?"

"Yes. You passed," Pete said, and then he told Daniel where to find Skylar.

"I have one more question. Did Skylar tell you herself or did someone else?"

"Skylar." Daniel didn't know how he felt about that, about the fact that his wife would call Pete instead of him. His conflict must have shown on his face, because Pete added, "I think she knew I'd tell you. I think she wanted me to."

"Why?"

"Because she loves you and she's miserable without you."

For the first time since Skylar'd left, Daniel felt hopeful.

The drummer of New Blues was a thirty-year-old named Eric Cleveland, and he hadn't blinked an eye when Skylar had showed up on his doorstep with her suitcase and her cat.

"Come on in. The guest bedroom's a mess, but you can tidy it up if it bothers you."

"It won't bother me."

"Didn't think so." Eric didn't mention Daniel, nor did he ask questions. He wasn't one to meddle in other people's business. He viewed life as a great big party and people as the partygoers, a diverse group he found endlessly fascinating. He wrote songs, he could harmonize any part and he played practically every instrument. He had talent coming out his ears and a generosity to match.

That's why Skylar had chosen him as her safe harbor instead of the lead guitarist Randy Tompkins, who lived in Huntsville with his wife and one child in a house that had two extra bedrooms and a guest bath.

She stowed her bag, fed her cat, then curled up on one end of the sofa with a diet soda and talked to Eric until three o'clock in the morning.

When she went to bed she was drained of everything except the need for sleep.

Chapter Forty

From the diary of Anne Beaufort Westmoreland:

October 10, 2001

Jake and Emily came in this morning to tell Michael about their wedding plans. Though none of us said anything, I believe we were all thinking the same thing: Michael's going to hear this and get so excited he'll wake up and say, "Why didn't somebody tell me this sooner?"

Well, anyhow...I thought Hannah was going to be here too, but she had something to do at the last minute. She didn't say what. I suspect it had something to do with her next assignment, and naturally I didn't ask questions. Not that it would have done any good. Hannah keeps things to herself. Always has. Even as a child.

I remember that time she fell out of a tree and broke her arm. It was three days before she ever told us, and I guess she wouldn't have then if the pain hadn't gotten so bad it scared her.

Back to this morning...I stood on one side of the bed holding Michael's hand and Em on the other doing the same thing.

"Dad, I have something important to tell you." That's the way she started, as if she were having an ordinary conversation with her father. Of all my children, Emily seems the most comfortable conversing with Michael. The most natural.

"Jake and I are not getting married in a church," she said. "We've decided to have the wedding at Base Camp Number Two in the Himalayas."

For a moment I thought Michael was going to come awake. I really did. His eyes sort of quivered, and I said, "That's it, darling. Go ahead. Wake up." But when I looked over at Emily and Jake I could see that they weren't excited about Michael: they were worried about me.

"Did you see that?" I said. "You saw how he tried to open his eyes, didn't you?"

Emily came around the bed and rested her cheek against mine. "Let's go outside for a minute, Mom."

I felt like an old woman when she led me out. I really did. And that makes me so mad I don't know what to do. Here's the way it is: As long as I had Michael I felt young and vibrant. Truly alive. But since he's been gone, since he's been sleeping, I've shriveled. I feel as if all my life's juices are being drained out of me. I feel as if I'm just a shell with skin stretched over it. Nothing underneath. Just half a heart that goes on beating.

Anyhow...out in the hallway my daughter told me

that yes, she'd hoped the excitement of returning to the Himalayas would cause Michael to come out of his coma. But all along she'd thought the chances were slim. "The real reason we've decided to be married there is that this whole family needs it. All of us need to go back and make peace with the mountain that took Dad away from us. But more than that I think we need to see what it was that kept drawing him back. You and I, most of all."

I was so proud of her I cried, and when she got anxious and said, "I'm going to call a nurse," I said, "No, no. I'm not upset. I'm happy."

Em laughed. God bless her heart, sometimes I think Emily understands me better than any of my children. I think she's more like me, too. Here we are, two women in love with men who will always be drawn to the high altitudes. Of course we need to stand face-to-face with the mountain. We need to hear the siren song that calls our men away.

Well, I don't know why she didn't tell me all that in Atlanta when she and Jake first shared their startling news. I guess she thought I'd figure it out for myself. Sometimes I think my children give me credit for having more sense than I actually do.

That's what I told Clarice when she came by to pick me up for lunch. "Anne, don't you know we're heroes to our children?" she told me, and I said, "I've never really thought about it, Clarice, you're the brain in this friendship," and she just cracked up. Lord, you could hear her laughing all over the restaurant. For about two minutes it was just like old times. I completely forgot that Michael was gone.

There now, I've said it. I've put it down in black and white and made it a fact. And it scares me to death.

It's getting harder and harder to look at this man sleeping in the bed and think of him as my husband. It's getting harder and harder to see this comatose form and remember how it was with Michael and me. The giddy feeling I got every time he walked into a room. The way he could drive me wild with nothing more than a touch on my cheek. Or a look. Lord, that man could just look at me and I'd feel as if I were melting all the way down to my toes.

That's another thing. I haven't bothered to paint my toenails since he's been gone. It brings back too many memories. And anyhow, why bother? Who's going to know? Who's going to care?

When I told Clarice, she didn't say a word, just picked up her purse and grabbed me by the arm and hauled me down the mall to the nearest walk-in salon. "Give my friend a pedicure and paint her toenails purple," she said.

That's why I'm sitting here now with my bare feet propped on Michael's bed and his hand resting on my left foot. I put it there, of course. A little while ago. And for just a moment it felt like old times. Michael was going to wake up and give me that wonderful smile, then reach for me and haul me up beside him and suck my toes.

Well, since I'm on such a soul-baring mission I'll have to admit what happened next. I came alive. Totally.

And now I know...I'm not wasting away inside. I'm merely dormant. Waiting for Michael to come back so I can come back to life.

Chapter Forty-One

I feel you, Anne. I always loved your feet—the shape of them, the astringent smell of fresh nail polish, the slenderness, the high arch.

I'm willing my muscles to move, willing them to let me bring your foot to my mouth and suck one of your delicate toes, to run my tongue between them and hear you make those delicious sounds as if I'm the world's sexiest man. That's how you made me feel. Did I ever tell you that? I hope so. In exactly those words.

Wait…I remember now. I always told you, you made me feel sixteen. That's it. You made me feel like a teenager full of energy and hormones.

I'm trying different ways to wake up. I can feel myself taking on energy. Almost as if I'm plugged in to some cosmic outlet. So far I haven't been able to control that energy, to direct it.

Right now I'm trying to direct all of it to my right hand. The one holding your left foot.

See…see how my cognitive abilities are coming back? I can tell this is your left foot because when you put my hand there you hooked my thumb under your arch.

Right now, lifting your foot is the most important thing in my life. The only thing. Not Em's wedding, though I would never tell her that. Not the thought of flying to the other side of the world to face once more the mountain that took me from you.

No, my world has become very small, my challenges reduced to the basics. Blink. Speak. Move.

Wait. There's something I'm missing. Something important.…

Telepathy. That's it. My mind is the one thing I have left that's fully functional. It's my one connection to you now. If I transmit my thoughts to you, will you receive them? We did it once. Now I wish we'd practiced more.

Here goes. I'm picturing myself out of this place and back home in Belle Rose. You're lying on the bed. I'm standing there undressing, and suddenly I can't wait that long. I bring your left foot to my mouth and suck your toes, one by one. Some I take deep, some shallow. An imitation of our lovemaking.

I feel your foot tense, then jerk. I hear those small sounds you're beginning to make. Soft. Urgent. Wait…don't stifle them with your hand. I want to hear.

Now I'm running my tongue into that sensitive space between your toes. Big toe first.

Ahhh. That's it. That's the sound I want to hear. The aftermath of a small explosion.

Go with it, Anne. Don't hold back. That's it. That's it,

my precious love. Feel my love pouring into you. Feel my desire, my need.

I need you, Anne. Bear with me. Bear with me a while longer.

I'm coming back to you. I'm coming home.

Chapter Forty-Two

Pete had driven all the way from Vicksburg, and was standing backstage with Skylar. Beyond the closed curtains she could hear the sounds of people coming into the auditorium.

"It's going to be a big crowd," she said, "Especially for such short notice."

"Who would pass up a chance to hear Skylar Tate in concert?" He squeezed her cold hands. "Are you nervous?"

"Yes."

She was thankful he didn't ask why. He didn't even act surprised. That was one reason she'd called to tell him about her plans. Pete was solid through and through. He hadn't tried to talk her out of putting together a benefit concert in only two days. He hadn't asked why she'd chosen a little country church in north Alabama as the recipient of all the proceeds. He hadn't questioned her wisdom in starting a foundation for wayward girls and naming it after her father.

Pete understood. Besides he had turned out to be the kind of man who could move mountains.

"I can't thank you enough for all your help, Pete."

"No thanks necessary. Just be happy, Skylar."

It was a strange way of saying good luck, but Skylar was too busy to think about it until the curtain went up and the stage lights came on. As she took her place in center stage the audience started clapping.

They hadn't come to hear speeches about a new charity named after a man they didn't even know. Some of them probably didn't even have a social conscience. They'd come to hear Skylar Tate sing.

Behind her Eric gave the cue, the band started to play, and Skylar started to sing. An old song. One of the hymns she'd sung when she was six years old and sitting on the front pew of the church dreading the moment her father ascended to the pulpit. He always insisted it be on a raised platform so folks had to look way up to him.

Skylar had hundreds of memories pasted into a mental scrapbook she'd carried around with her for years. Tonight she was shutting it up and putting it away. Tonight she was singing the old songs in a new way. Free and easy and from the heart.

As her eyes adjusted to the lights she began to pick out faces in the audience. There was Pete in the third row. Randy Tompkins's wife was sitting two rows back. She'd brought Nancy, their oldest child, sixteen and already showing her dad's talent.

Skylar's gaze swung to the right. There was the man from the service station. Carl. And behind him was...her husband.

Skylar almost faltered. She almost forgot the lyrics. The only thing that saved her was her professionalism.

Daniel was in Atlanta. That had to be someone who looked like him. Her mind was playing tricks.

She walked stage right to get a better look, and Daniel gave her that unforgettable smile, the one she could conjure up in an instant, the one that had followed her all the way from Atlanta, Georgia, to Huntsville, Alabama. The one that would follow her to the ends of the earth.

She would have done the entire first set standing on stage right drinking in the sight of her husband except for the fact that she was here to entertain.

Skylar crossed to stage left with a new bounce in her step. As always when she was performing, she lost all count of time. Music flowed from her. And when she left the stage, the spotlight followed her until she disappeared into the wings.

Pete was standing there to hand her a towel. "Thanks." She kissed his cheek. "I didn't even see you leave."

"I guess not." He grinned. "He's waiting for you in the dressing room. Take your time. If you're not back, the band can start the second set with Eric's new songs. This would be as good a time as any to give them a test run."

If Skylar hadn't been so nervous she'd have raced back to her dressing room the minute she heard Daniel was waiting, but for the first time in her life she felt shy and uncertain. What was she going to say to him? What would he say to her? After all, she was the one who'd left. His smile could mean everything...or nothing. Daniel was a friendly man. He smiled at everybody.

"You're making sounds like a manager, Pete...I hope." She and the other members of the band had been thinking of changing managers for quite some time.

"Could be." He nodded toward the dressing room. "Go

on, Skylar. You have better things to do than stand here gabbing with me.''

''Thanks, Pete. For everything.'' She took a deep breath. ''Wish me luck.''

''You don't need it, Sky. You have everything you need right here.'' He put his hand on her heart, then gave her a little push. ''Knock 'em dead, beautiful.''

Daniel couldn't pray, he couldn't think, he couldn't do anything except pace. What if Hannah had been wrong about him doing this alone? What if Skylar took one look at him and slammed the door? What if Pete told her he was waiting and she didn't even show up?

What if...?

The door opened and there she was. His wife. The woman he loved more than life itself. The most magnificent, most remarkable woman he'd ever met.

He couldn't lose her again. He *wouldn't* lose her again.

''You were great, Sky.''

''Thanks.''

She hovered near the doorway and Daniel realized she was as unsure of her footing as he. Was that a good thing or a bad thing? He didn't know. All he knew was how much he wanted to touch her.

They stared at each other for a small eternity. Daniel couldn't get enough of looking at her. The tight red-sequined dress clung to the curves he knew so well, and perspiration shone on the skin he'd kissed a thousand times.

The skin he was going to kiss again. Without thinking of the consequences, Daniel closed the distance between them and took her in his arms. She gave a startled gasp and opened her mouth to say something but Daniel never heard what it was. He was too busy kissing her.

And she was kissing him back. That was the main thing.

His wife was kissing him back without hesitation and without reserve. Suddenly Daniel knew paradise. It was here, in this room in Huntsville, Alabama.

He molded her to his body and marveled once again at how well they fit. Always had, always would. There could never be another woman for him. There could be no life for him without Skylar, for his heart was irrevocably bound with hers.

All he had to do was convince her.

They kissed until their lips felt bruised and puffy. They kissed until they had merged so close together you couldn't tell where one body left off and the other started. They might have kissed forever if Skylar hadn't felt the burden of things not spoken.

"Daniel..." She leaned back to look at him, and *Oh, that was love she saw in his eyes, his face. It had to be.* "There are some things we need to talk about."

"Yes." He took her hand and led her to the only chair in the room, then knelt in front of her, still holding her hand.

It felt wonderful. And she realized what she'd almost lost, what she could lose again if she weren't careful. She brought his hand to her lips and kissed each knuckle with such reverence he got tears in his eyes.

"I didn't want to leave you, please understand that."

"I know. Your note made that clear."

"Good." She sighed. All the things she should say raced around her mind, squirrel-like, and she couldn't seem to get them organized.

"You have a show to finish, Sky. We can talk later."

"There's no hurry. I won't be able to sing unless I know why you're here."

"To take you home with me...if you want to go."

Relief settled over her, warm and comforting, and suddenly she could breathe again.

"Yes…oh, yes. I want to go home."

She couldn't bear another moment without being in his arms. They reached for each other at the same time and ended up on the floor kissing as if the world were coming to an end and they'd have to wait till the next lifetime to get another chance.

Skylar didn't know whether she'd tumbled or Daniel had pulled her off the chair; the thing that mattered was his lips on hers. His hands were all over her and she thought she would die of happiness.

Outside their little spot of heaven the band filed back onstage, and faint strains of music drifted around them. Blues. Music of the heart. Music of the soul.

Daniel leaned back a fraction of an inch. "You have to go back."

"Not yet. Not for another thirty minutes or so." She ran her hands inside his shirt and tangled her fingers in the crisp chest hair she loved so well.

"Sky…" His voice had dropped half an octave to that deep sexy timbre that made her shiver.

"The door's locked," she whispered, then reached for his belt buckle.

When Daniel slid into his seat, Hannah whispered, "You're late."

He grinned at her and said, "I know."

She leaned back to take a good look at him, and even though it was mostly dark in the auditorium Daniel figured his face still glowed with love, for his sister's smile got so wide it made him think of the Cheshire cat.

"Good," she said, then settled back into her seat just as Skylar Tate Westmoreland took the stage.

She didn't need spotlights. The glow in her face was enough. Daniel settled back to enjoy the show. *Really* enjoy it. Now that he knew how it would all turn out, now that he knew his quest was over, he could pay attention to songs Sky sang, to the way she was singing them.

She sang with a new power. A freedom that made the music soar. He was her biggest fan. He'd always admired her talent and enjoyed her music.

But this was different. This music mesmerized, hypnotized. He was aware of nothing except the woman and the music.

If he had never heard her sing he would have given all the credit to the rousing lovemaking they'd enjoyed in her dressing room. The marvelous welcome-back-home way they'd greeted each other.

But Daniel sensed something different about his wife. A new spark. A magic.

The audience did, too, for although many of the songs she sang were different from her recordings, they responded with wild enthusiasm that at times bordered on frenzy.

Skylar sang until almost midnight, and the crowd kept calling for more. Daniel could see how sweat glistened on her face and in her cleavage. But he saw no waning of energy, no signs of fatigue.

"She's absolutely marvelous," Hannah said.

"Yes, she is."

"I've never heard anything like her." Hannah swiveled in her seat to study him. "You know what this means, don't you, Daniel?"

"Yes." To take her away from the entertainment world would be almost a sacrilege. He'd always understood that. But his sister had to make certain.

"Don't domesticate her."

"I won't even try."

Skylar wound up her final song, then held her arms up in appeal to a crowd that still called for more.

"One more encore," she said, and the crowd went wild. She smiled, waiting for them to calm down, then she came to the edge of the proscenium and said, "But first I have someone I want to introduce to you. Someone very special. My husband."

Nothing in his ministry had prepared Daniel for the kind of scrutiny he endured as he wove his way through the crowd. When he took his place on stage and put his arm around Skylar, the audience went wild once more, yelling and stomping and clapping.

He looked across the crowd till he found his sister. Hannah was enjoying every minute of it.

Skylar held up her hands once more. "I want all of you to meet my husband, the Reverend Daniel Westmoreland."

Hushed silence fell over the crowd, then as the shock wore off they went into another frenzy of stomping and yelling and clapping. Tonight Skylar Tate could do no wrong.

"I didn't know you were going to do that," Daniel said.

They'd talked briefly about the introduction. After he'd zipped her into a green-sequined gown that matched her eyes, she'd asked, "Do you mind if I tell them you're my husband?" and he'd said, "I would be honored."

That was all.

Now she leaned close to him and said, "You've let me have my identity. How can I not do the same for you?"

That's when he kissed her. And she kissed him. They didn't even know when the crowd finally quit clapping and went on home.

The only encore she got around to was the one in her dressing room with Daniel.

Chapter Forty-Three

Room 414 at the Marriott was filled with flowers. Skylar went from one bouquet to the other inhaling the fragrance while Daniel watched her.

"You did all this for me," she said.

"Yes."

"Even though you weren't sure I'd come."

"I knew you would come back to me."

She laced her arms around his neck and pulled him close. "How did you know?"

"Because we belong together."

The truth of what he said was in Skylar's heart, and she knew that if Daniel had not come to her, she would have gone back to him. No matter what the consequences.

"Daniel, I know it's late but we have to talk. I'd like very much to do it before I sleep. In fact, I'm not sure I can sleep."

"I don't intend for you to," he said, and she felt as

flushed as if this would be their first time together. He led her to the sofa, then opened the curtains so they could see the Saturn 5 rocket lit up and reaching toward the sky.

"You don't mind, do you?"

"It's one way to ensure that we talk instead of do delicious things to each other." She nabbed a sofa cushion and stuck it behind her back, then Daniel pulled her feet into his lap and began to massage them.

"Comfortable?"

"Very."

"What do you want to talk about first?"

"You. What happened at the meeting? I hope they weren't too hard on you."

"Just the opposite. The newspaper article stirred their compassion. They offered their apologies and their support. They asked how they could make it up to you."

Skylar couldn't speak around the lump in her throat. Daniel reached over and wiped her tears with his fingertips, then pulled her into his lap and kissed the rest of them away.

"So you see, Sky, you didn't have to run at all."

She couldn't answer for a long while because his mouth covered hers. "Yes, I did," she said, finally. "I had to run because of me. I had to come back here and confront my past in order to be free."

"You're free now, Sky. And safe. You don't ever have to run again."

"Yes, I know." As she rubbed her cheek against his chest she thought about how far she'd come—from the defiant woman hiding the scared little girl inside, to a contented woman who wasn't afraid of anything anymore, including letting the child inside her come out to play.

"Daniel, can you carry me to bed?"

"Certainly." He swept her up and said, "Just right. A

woman I can carry around.'' Then he dumped her on the bed where she bounced, laughing. Daniel was already headed toward the windows to close the curtains.

"Leave them," she said. "I want to see the rocket."

"My competition." He left a trail of clothes as he came back to the bed.

"I wouldn't worry if I were you. I think you're equal to the task."

"You'd better show me," he said.

And she did.

Chapter Forty-Four

They all left today for the Himalayas—Anne, Hannah, Daniel, Skylar, Emily and Jake. I wish I could have gone with them. I tried. I really did try.

Anne almost backed out at the last minute. She said, "I can't leave Michael alone like this," and Clarice told her, "He's not alone, he's with me, and if you don't get out of here I'm going to whip your butt."

Clarice is here with me now. I can smell her perfume and hear the bangles on her wrist every time she moves her arms. I'm glad Anne has her.

When I wake up I'm going to do something special for her to show my appreciation. I can't think what right now. But it will come to me.

Everything seems to be coming back to me. I have devised a method of keeping track of time. Since I'm in a cave of sorts I've imagined a sharp stone I can hold in my hand and use to mark off the days. Amazing how it works.

All I have to do is call up that cave wall and I see the series of marks I've made.

For instance, I know that today is October thirteenth. The wedding is on the seventeenth, and Anne will be back the nineteenth. Six days. A whirlwind trip.

She'll be exhausted. I wish she would stay longer. I wish I could have told her, Take all the time you need, angel. Don't hurry back on my account. I'll be right here. Waiting for you.

I can tell by the sounds outside in the hall that it will soon be dark. Clarice is getting restless and anxious to go home. She has a new boyfriend. I know this from her conversations with Anne. She'll soon leave and I'll be alone for the first time since the accident.

Truly alone.

That scares me. If I stay in this coma much longer, Anne will have to resume her life. She won't be around day and night talking to me, holding me, loving me.

I can't let that happen. I won't let that happen.

While she's gone I'm going to do my best to wake up. I'm going to use every ounce of willpower I have to get out of this bed and surprise her.

That would be a wonderful homecoming. For both of us.

Chapter Forty-Five

They approached the Himalayas on the Nepalese side. From the moment the peak had come into sight, Michael Westmoreland's family had fallen silent. They were under the spell of the mountain.

It affected each one of them differently. Jake became energized, which is what Daniel would expect from his future brother-in-law. Jake had climbing in his blood just as Michael did. Mountains would always lure him. He would always climb, but probably not without Emily.

What surprised Daniel was her obvious eagerness for this high-altitude adventure. He could imagine how she would choose to climb with her husband. Not all the time but enough so that the mountains wouldn't separate them for long stretches of time the way they had her mother and father.

Then there was Hannah. She faced the mountain with fierceness and determination, in typical Hannah fashion.

But there was something else, too. An inner rage that Daniel had hoped would have abated by now.

He knew that he felt none. The mountain no longer seemed the enemy it had when it first took Michael's ordinary life and cast him into a world of deep sleep. It was neither friend nor foe. Neither benevolent nor angry. It was awesome in its power and grandeur.

For the first time in his life he understood why his father had to climb. He understood why his father had left his family for weeks at a time in order to challenge the mountain. Just as Daniel found what he was seeking in the church, Michael found it on the mountain.

And both of them were right.

Skylar squeezed Daniel's hand, and he glanced at his wife. She was feeling the same thing. He could tell by the look on her face. And tonight when they lay side by side in their tent, curved close against each other in the sleeping bag, they would talk about the mountain in awed whispers.

He squeezed her hand right back, then leaned over and kissed her.

His mother saw them and smiled. She was the one who had surprised Daniel most. He didn't know what he'd expected—a few tears, perhaps, or at least a bone-deep sadness. Instead the mountain had an uplifting effect on Anne. It was as if she understood for the first time what had happened to Michael and why. It was as if she were shedding some great burden she'd carried on her shoulders, placing it at the foot of the mountain and saying, "Here, you can have it now. I've finished with it."

"We'll pitch camp here," their Nepalese guide told them, and they all got busy setting up their tents for the night.

Tomorrow they would reach their destination, Base Camp Number Two which was a modest climb and easily attainable, even for those who had never climbed, which was all of them except Jake and the guide.

Night came quickly in the Himalayas. One minute it was light, and the next a black curtain dropped down and they all went inside their tents to rest from the day's hike and prepare themselves for tomorrow's climb.

Skylar wrapped her arms around Daniel, cuddled close and wet his chest with her tears.

"What's wrong, Sky?"

"It's not what's wrong; it's what's right. Oh, Daniel..." She sighed and inched closer. "This mountain feels sacred to me. Do you feel that?"

"Yes. Reaching the peak must have been a spiritual experience for Dad."

"Hmmm." They lay quietly together while the stars lit the night sky. They seemed brighter in the mountains. Closer.

"Daniel," Skylar whispered. "When two people truly love each other, showing that love in a physical way is the most spiritual experience I know."

Daniel shifted them, and when he entered her, he whispered, "I truly love you, Sky."

It was a long, long while before either of them could speak, and then she said, "I truly love you, too."

The wedding party wore ski pants and thermal underwear. They stood in a tight circle around the bride and groom, who held hands and smiled at each other. The sheer ice-covered face of the mountain was their cathedral, and a boulder was their altar.

Daniel stood in front of the boulder to officiate his sister's wedding. He didn't ask, Who giveth this woman to be married to this man? Everyone knew the answer to that question.

Michael gave his daughter to Jake. No one else could take his place, and no one else attempted it.

Emily and Jake were waiting. Daniel looked out over the mountain for a moment, searching, and then placed his hand over theirs and began.

"Dearly beloved, we are gathered here today to celebrate the wedding of Emily and Jake..."

A chilled breeze touched the back of his neck and he looked up at the circle of family. The empty space beside Anne suddenly glowed, filled with sunlight. And inside that light appeared the figure of a man. He reached for Anne's hand, and he was smiling.

Daniel didn't speak of what he'd seen on the mountain. They hiked back down and put Anne on a plane going home.

Emily and Jake flew out that same day for a honeymoon trip to Venice. Hannah left for her assignment while Daniel and Skylar stayed behind for a long-delayed *real* honeymoon.

They took a hotel room with wide windows facing the Himalayas. Two days after the wedding they lay in bed holding each other and watching the sunrise. It started on the highest peak and descended the mountain, lighting each face on its descent.

Neither of them spoke until a golden light filled the room.

"Did you see it?" Skylar asked, and Daniel knew instinctively that she wasn't talking about the sunrise.

"Yes. I saw it."

"What do you think it was?"

"Not what. Who."

Skylar leaned on her elbow so she could look at him. "Then it *was* the figure of a man?"

"Yes, it was my father."

She shivered as if she were suddenly cold, and he wrapped her closer.

"If anything had happened to him, we would have heard. Right?"

"Yes. Dad's okay."

"Then, what was it, Daniel?"

"I don't know. I think that his love for Mom is so strong he found a way to send his spirit here to be with her."

He traced his wife's breasts with his fingertips, reveling in the familiar feel of her soft skin, delighting in the way she became instantly aroused. And he knew beyond a shadow of a doubt that he had found the kind of love his father and mother had. He knew that no matter what happened, no matter where her career took her or his took him, they would always be together.

"Love me, Daniel." Skylar shifted on top of him, and as he slid home he said, "Always, my love. Always."

Chapter Forty-Six

From the diary of Anne Beaufort Westmoreland:

October 19, 2001

I'm sitting here in seat 2B sipping a Baileys and coffee and trying to remember every detail of Emily's wedding so I won't leave out a thing when I tell Michael. Also, I want to record everything that happened just in case...

Well, I'm not even going to finish that thought. When you're more than thirty thousand feet in the air, the last thing you should think about is being caught in your own tragedy. One in the family is enough.

Oh, I know, I know. I have to quit thinking of what's happened to Michael as a current tragedy. The worst part is over—seeing him like that. God help me, I'm getting used to it. But I don't like it, not one little bit, and I refuse to accept it. I guess I'm a bit of a Southern belle after all, a bit like Scarlett when she went into the radish patch and swore to the Almighty that she would never be hungry again.

Well, I'm swearing here and now that I will *never* accept Michael's absence. Swearing it in purple ink. I'm going to bring him back even if I have to comb the ends of the earth to find a way to do it.

One thing I have to do is be more optimistic and less warrior-like. Clarice tells me that all the time. She knows because she reads all kinds of books about positive thinking and Eastern philosophies with names I can't even pronounce. Of course, I could if I wanted to, but I always say that to Clarice because she gets such a kick out of being smart.

God bless her for staying with my Michael. If she hadn't I couldn't have gone, but I can tell you the honest truth. I can barely endure being apart from him. Every part of my body aches for him, every muscle, every sinew, every bone. There hasn't been a single day that I didn't yearn for him with such a fierceness I thought I'd break apart in a million pieces.

I can't wait to see him again, to hold him, to kiss him, to tell him I love him. No, I don't merely love him. He's my heart, my life, my entire universe.

Oh God...

Well, I certainly made a fool of myself right here in the first-class section of the airplane. But I don't care. Not one bit. I got to missing Michael so much I started crying into my Baileys and coffee. Two flight attendants came over to pamper me, and it felt good. They gave me scented tissues and got a cool cloth to wash my face, then fixed me a fresh coffee. I guess all that attention worked because I'm feeling better now and am writing once more. Trying to get it all down. The wedding, but first the mountain.

I can hardly find the words to describe how I felt when I first saw the summit of Everest rising out of the mists. The most formidable of all mountains was suddenly before me and I didn't think about Michael's accident at all. I was wonder-struck by its magnificence and spellbound by its power. I literally felt a tug as if this awesome mountain were exerting some sort of magnetic power over me.

I know that's what Michael felt. Without even asking I know that's why he kept going back.

I'll have to ask him when he returns to me.

That's how I'm thinking of him now. Not as being asleep and getting ready to wake up, but as being gone and getting ready to come back.

I know he's coming back to me because he came to the mountain. I didn't tell any of the children this, but Michael was there at Emily's wedding. Not the whole time, and not right away.

He wasn't in the Himalayas when we first arrived, nor on the climb to Base Camp. He wasn't there beside me as I slept under the stars, awestruck by the same view he's had dozens of times.

No, my husband didn't appear until Daniel started the wedding ceremony. Then suddenly there was Michael. Standing beside me.

I felt him before I saw him. Felt a whisper of a breeze against my cheek, like a caress. And then there was a brilliance unlike anything I've seen. It filled the empty space I'd insisted we leave in the circle. Michael's space.

And I knew it was him. Knew it before I saw the shadow. Knew it in my heart.

Then he reached out and caught my hand. I knew it

was him. No one has hands quite as beautiful as my Michael. Quite as strong. Quite as wonderful.

I shivered when he touched me. I shiver still, just thinking about it.

You're here, my darling, I wanted to say, but I didn't. The children would have thought I'd gone mad. And perhaps I have. Perhaps this longing for his return has driven me over the brink.

But I don't think so. Oh, I don't think so.

Here's what I believe, what I know...there is a mystical connection between Michael and me, one that transcends time and space. For we are not only husband and wife in this life, but we've been lovers through the ages, true soul mates who will always find each other, no matter where we are, no matter what the circumstances, no matter what the time.

Michael is my destiny and I am his. I know this truth deep in my bones.

There's another truth I know: He's coming back to me.... Michael will always return to me.

* * * * *

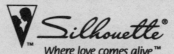

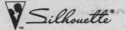

SPECIAL EDITION™

Save $1.00 off your purchase of any Silhouette Special Edition® title

Experience it all with Silhouette Special Edition®—
life, love and family!

For an emotional, compelling read that captures the
intensity of living, loving and creating a family in
today's world, pick up a Special Edition novel.

$1.00 OFF!
your purchase of any
Silhouette Special Edition® title!

RETAILER: Harlequin Enterprises Ltd. will pay the face value of this coupon plus 8¢ if
submitted by customer for this product only. Any other use constitutes fraud. Coupon is
nonassignable. Void if taxed, prohibited or restricted by law. Consumer must pay any
government taxes. Valid in U.S. only. For reimbursement submit coupons and proof of sales
to: Harlequin Enterprises Ltd., P.O. Box 880478, El Paso, TX 88588-0478, U.S.A. Cash value
1/100¢. Limit one coupon per purchase. Redeemable at participating retailers.

108052

Coupon expires July 31, 2002.
Valid at retail outlets in U.S. only.

5 65373 00076 2   (8100) 0 10805

Where love comes alive™

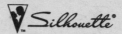

SPECIAL EDITION™

Save $1.00 off your purchase of any Silhouette Special Edition® title

Experience it all with Silhouette Special Edition®—
life, love and family!

For an emotional, compelling read that captures the
intensity of living, loving and creating a family in
today's world, pick up a Special Edition novel.

$1.00 OFF!
your purchase of any
Silhouette Special Edition® title!

Silhouette®

```
52603916
```

Silhouette®
Where love comes alive™

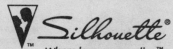